ICE
WARRIOR

BOOKS BY RUTH RIDDELL

Haunted Journey
Shadow Witch
Ice Warrior

ICE WARRIOR

RUTH RIDDELL

ATHENEUM · 1992 · NEW YORK
Maxwell Macmillan Canada
TORONTO
Maxwell Macmillan International
NEW YORK   OXFORD   SINGAPORE   SYDNEY

Atheneum
Macmillan Publishing Company
866 Third Avenue
New York, NY 10022

Maxwell Macmillan Canada, Inc.
1200 Eglinton Avenue East
Suite 200
Don Mills, Ontario M3C 3N1

Macmillan Publishing Company is part of the Maxwell Communication Group of Companies.

First edition

Printed in the United States of America

10 9 8 7 6 5 4 3 2 1

The text of this book is set in Bodoni Book.

Book design by Patrice Fodero.

LIBRARY OF CONGRESS CATALOGING-IN-PUBLICATION DATA

Riddell, Ruth.
    Ice Warrior / Ruth Riddell.
        p.   cm.
    Summary: When his mother's remarriage moves him from sunny California to snowy Minnesota, twelve-year-old Rob feels totally out of place until he discovers iceboating, which he hopes will be the means to prove himself to his highly competitive father.
    ISBN 0–689–31710–7
    [1. Iceboating—Fiction. 2. Minnesota—Fiction. 3. Remarriage—Fiction.
    4. Fathers and sons—Fiction.] I. Title.
    PZ7.R4166Ic—1992
    [Fic]—dc20   91–29506

*For all the dads and
for all the sons who love them*

Success should not be based on how much one achieves. Rather it should be based on the number of obstacles one overcomes to achieve.

CHAPTER 1

Rob sat on the edge of his bed, studying the hurriedly written note. "Rob," it began. "I'll be in Minneapolis first week in February for important meeting. Will drive to Welholm Falls Saturday morning." It was signed "Dad."

Rob folded the paper in half. He creased it several times, then used his fingernail to crease it again. "Great"—he expelled a deep breath—"just great."

Rob moved across the room. He paused to study the stack of schoolbooks, then looked out at the foot of snow covering the earth, the dark clouds overhead, the icicles hanging from the roof of the house next door. His dad and California seemed like a place on the other side of the world.

Rob returned to his bed, dropped down, and read the note again. He wanted to see his dad. The past five months seemed like five years. Then why was he feeling so miserable?

1

"Rob"—the voice came up the stairway—"it's time to go."

Once again he looked at the note, then across the room to the photograph—his dad, his mom, and himself when he was a little kid. Rob could hardly remember being that small. He could hardly remember his mom and dad looking that happy.

"Rob"—the voice grew impatient—"you're going to be late."

Rob aimed the note toward his desk. He threw it like a Frisbee. He watched it hit the stack of schoolbooks, bounce back, slip into the trash basket beside the list of incomplete assignments.

"Rob!"

"I'm coming," he called. "I'll be right there."

As Rob moved toward the door, he gathered up skates, stick, and helmet. He grabbed a doughnut as he hurried through the kitchen. He had a bad feeling about the afternoon game, a feeling that continued to worsen during the drive to the arena, during warm-ups and well into the third period. Though he disliked sitting on the bench and being third string, when Jerry Canady went down and Coach Enge motioned Rob onto the ice, he cringed.

The Polar Bears were a cinch for division champions if they beat the Demmering Eskimos. Rob pushed up from his place on the lonely end of the bench. He skated past the other guys. He knew them as second- and third-stringers. They knew him as the new kid, the kid whose mom married the high school coach, the guy with two left feet and a sunbaked brain.

2

"Rob"—Coach Enge slid an arm across Rob's shoulders—"watch Five; he's shifty and quick."

Rob put on his helmet, fastened the chin strap. This had to be the dumbest thing he had ever had to do. He was a warm weather kid, windsurfing was his thing, the *Sun Warrior* his magic. He grew up with sandy beaches, palm trees, and sunshine. Hockey sticks, ice skates, shin guards—all his new dad's idea. "Everyone in Welholm Falls plays hockey. It will be an easy way for you to make new friends."

Easy had quickly turned into *disastrous*. Not only was his mind stuck in low gear but his ankles behaved like overcooked spaghetti. Rob moved into position. Smitty came up from the defense zone. "Watch Five; he's a mean machine."

Five . . . the Eskimos' leading scorer . . . built like a blockhouse . . . clever with his stick and playing the innocent act.

Rob scowled. He puffed out his chest. He tried to act tough, bigger than he was—a ninety-pound marshmallow on skates. Stay cool, he told himself. We're leading, six to five . . . three minutes left. No problem.

But Rob knew that the Demmering Eskimos were a strong team and capable of beating the Polar Bears. Number Five could strike from anywhere on the ice. Rob tried to swallow, but a couple hundred butterflies turned his belly into a three-ring circus.

The referee skated in to drop the puck. Brian Sass played center for the Polar Bears and stood a head taller than most of his teammates; nearly twice Rob's size. But size had nothing to do with Sass's threatening glance. Brian was a real hockey player, a serious competitor. He insisted on winning and his glance told Rob that he had better not make a mistake. The referee blew his whistle, the puck fell, sticks hit. Sass sent the disk back to Charlie Ellis. But Eskimo Number Five drove in, deflected the puck in Rob's direction. Rob scooped it up, pivoted to avoid Five's rush. He took off, moved ahead. He saw Brian open in the middle and fired a perfect pass. Sass yelled out the signal for power play "Red." Rob circled behind the net, ready to slap the puck in behind the goalie if Brian should miss. But Sass feinted one way, fired the opposite, and the buzzer went off. The score changed, seven to five, and the butterflies churning inside Rob's stomach quieted. As Rob skated into position, he saw his mom in the stands, his new dad, his stepbrother, Doug, and two of his buddies. All three played high school hockey; all three had been Polar Bears. It seemed to Rob that every male in Welholm Falls had been a Polar Bear. Would they expect him to play mistake-free, when his only experience on skates had been in a rink called the Sunny California Ice Palace? If he messed up, would his mom be embarrassed?

Rob glanced at the time clock. Two minutes. Just two minutes. Could he finish the period without making a critical error? At least, Rob thought, his dad wouldn't see him mess up.

Both teams huddled. Sass called the play and shot Rob a worried look. "Watch Five," Brian warned. "He thinks his guys can beat us and he'll do his best to pull one of us out of position. You guys stay in your own lanes."

The Polar Bears broke; each moved to his spot on the ice. As soon as the puck dropped, Five slapped it back to Seven. Sass started to pursue the puck, but Five checked him hard. The rest of the Eskimos came across center ice like an assault force. Rob moved back, careful to stay in his lane. The puck caught him looking as it whizzed by. Rob followed it into the boards, dug it out, drew back to fire, but Five's elbow came up under Rob's chin and sent him reeling into the boards.

Rob recovered and went after Five. He'd give the Eskimo center an elbow he wouldn't forget. But the moment Rob committed to center ice, Seven slanted into Rob's unprotected area, took a backhanded shot from Five, and raced ahead, untouched.

The mistake! Rob spun around. He tried to recover. He chased the play. Seven slipped the puck down the right side. Rob stuck out his stick but the puck whistled past. Nine picked it up, dumped it off to Five who centered it back to Seven. Seven slashed inside. Brian followed him to the boards but missed Seven's slapshot. Nine gathered in the puck, then fired a red-hot sizzler across to Five. A hole opened in the middle. Rob powered inside, stole the puck. But his theft lasted only a moment. Five checked Rob to his knees. Seven came alongside and spun Rob around. Five tripped, fell on top of Rob, his knee pinning Rob's twisted ankle. Five bounced back, took off toward the play in front of the Polar Bears' net. Rob tried to pull up but went down a second time; the pain in his ankle shot through his body. Tears washed over his eye.

The Eskimos scored.

Silence gripped the Polar Bears' fans, while the opposing team went wild. The Eskimos had a chance now. The Polar Bears' lead shrank to one. And Rob wanted to die.

He raised himself onto a knee, then to one foot, balanced himself on his stick. "You okay?" Smitty asked.

Coach Enge motioned Rob off the ice; Canady limped in. "Let me give you a hand," Smitty said.

But Rob shook him away. He wanted to disappear, evaporate. At least his dad had not been in the stands to see his stupid mistake. Rob hobbled back to his place at the empty end of the bench.

The Eskimos struck quickly and tied the score. Just before the final buzzer, Five took a short pass from Seven, raced the length of the ice, and scored. Spectators from Demmering went wild while everyone from Welholm Falls filed out quietly. The locker room sounded like a tomb except for Brian Sass. He slammed his helmet to the floor, kicked the wooden bench, and punched the locker door.

"That ankle looks mighty swollen." Coach Enge sat beside Rob. "Can you stand on it?"

Rob nodded. "I'm sorry I messed up. I got sore when that—"

"No need to apologize. This is your first season. Isn't a boy in this room that hasn't lost his temper and made the same mistake."

Enge ruffled Rob's hair. "We still have a shot at the championship. Sorry that you won't be able to play with us."

"I'll be fine. A few days off my ankle and . . . Coach, I can play."

His dad was coming to town; he had to play. But Coach Enge said, "That's a bad sprain, Rob. It'll take longer to heal than a few days. How 'bout a ride home?"

Rob shook his head. "Some of the guys—" He glanced over his shoulder. Smitty went out the door first. Sass hurried Ellis and Canady out next.

When the cold, late afternoon air hit Rob, he caught his breath. The pain from his ankle shot up into his heart and threatened to crush it as he watched the guys run ahead. They could have asked him along . . . they could have, but they hadn't.

Rob pulled his coat collar around his ears as wind swept across the lake. Ice particles stung his wet cheeks. "Stupid ankle," he shouted, and limped his way across the south end of the lake. On the other side he stopped to study the poster nailed to a telephone pole. A figure of a hockey player, crouched and ready to score, stared back at him.

WINTER FESTIVAL; FIRST WEEKEND IN FEBRUARY
HOCKEY GAMES, DOG SLEDDING, SKIJORING,
ICEBOATING, SNOWMOBILE RACES
PRIZES, TROPHIES, FUN FOR EVERYONE.

Rob thought about his dad. If *he* lived in Welholm Falls, he'd win it all. Larry Marshall was good at everything. A natural athlete, fierce competitor. Nothing ever stood in his way. "Winning isn't everything, Rob. It's the only thing."

7

Rob turned up Lakefront Drive. It was a wide street. Large lawns surrounded each old house, all in a row. So different from the modern hillside house his parents once shared—ice plant instead of grass, eucalyptus trees instead of maples, sunshine instead of cold, gray skies and the icy wind that blew against him now.

His mom said he had to accept the divorce, accept her marriage to Jim Erikson, accept Welholm Falls, accept a new school and new friends.

Rob crossed Seventh toward the old three-story white house where he now lived. He glanced at the house next door where Jennifer lived, saw her standing in the window, waving. He waved back glumly. Probably everyone in Jennifer's family already knew that he was the cause of the Polar Bears' losing.

Jennifer was born in Welholm Falls. She knew everyone. Everyone knew her. Her mother was the town librarian and her dad sold insurance. Jennifer was the smartest girl Rob had ever known. She finished her math assignments first, wrote the best science reports, read faster than anyone else in Rob's seventh-grade class. Besides, she was his friend, the only real friend he had here. Last summer when he'd first moved to Welholm Falls, she'd invited him to go swimming and bicycling, to the movies and fishing with her family.

Rob hesitated alongside the Johannsens' mailbox. Jennifer would have finished the math assignments and every answer would be right. If she knew, Rob reasoned, that his were still there to do, she might volunteer her papers.

Rob brushed the snow from the top of the Johannsens' mailbox. He could walk up to her door, knock. He could tell her the good news, that his dad was coming to visit. He could mention the math assignments. . . . But Jennifer would want to hear more about the hockey game, why he was limping, why he wasn't off having pizza with the guys.

Rob blew his breath into the empty space. He muttered that borrowing her math papers was a dumb idea and turned up the driveway to his home.

His mother called the three-story house a "Victorian with charm." Built years ago by his new dad's grandfather. Jim had been born in the house, married his first wife in the living room. "A house with lots of family tradition," his mother had told him. She called it "lovely, a joy to care for, fun to redecorate."

And she had done just that after she married Jim. Painted or wallpapered every room, hung new curtains, made slipcovers for all the downstairs furniture. Doug called the changes "terrific." Jim said, "It's been a long time since the old place has felt a woman's touch."

Rob guessed all the changes were okay. The polished wood floors were neat for sliding on in his socks, and the banister—a straight shot from the second-floor landing to the entryway. Jim said, "There's not been an Erikson who hasn't given that banister a slide."

Rob stared at the ruffled white curtains crisscrossing the floor-to-ceiling bow window. Thoughts of the unfinished homework—the end of Christmas vacation, the Polar Bears' loss, and an ankle that would keep him from playing the remainder of the season—told him he was a failure. But it was his dad's visit that made him want to cry.

CHAPTER 2

Rob slid from his place on the bed, hopped across to the television, turned it off, then hopped back. He pushed his foot and swollen ankle deeper into the bucket of ice water because Jim had said it was the best thing to do for a sprain.

Rob knew he should be working on his math instead of thinking about his dad's visit and the end of hockey season. He hated math, especially fractions, and Brian Sass was a—

"Hey, Squirt"—Doug's voice flew into the room at the same time the door opened—"dinner's ready. How's the ankle?"

Everyone in Welholm Falls knew Doug Erikson. During hockey season his picture appeared on the weekly sports page. And he owned a shelfful of trophies that proved he was the best at hockey, tennis, wrestling, almost everything. "I'm not hungry," Rob answered.

"Not hungry?" Doug straddled the desk chair. "Your mom is one terrific cook. How come you're not hungry?"

Rob kept looking at the columns of fractions until Doug asked, "You going to practice tomorrow?"

"Coach says I'm done for the season. Doug"—Rob raised his math book from the pillow—"could you help me understand this stuff?"

Doug leaned forward. "Fractions? Not me, Buddy, but Dad's a whiz. Come on, let's eat."

"Maybe later."

Except for the sound of the door closing, the latch snapping, quiet reached into every corner of the room. The desk lamp filled the space with shadows. Rob focused on the dark window while his thoughts carried him back to California, to the *Sun Warrior* and windsurfing, to an occasional Sunday afternoon when his dad had an extra ticket and took him along to see the Chargers play.

Rob fell back against his pillow. His dad would be visiting when everyone in town was participating in some festival event, everyone but him. What would his dad think of his son, the spectator? Would he understand or would he—

Before he could answer his own question, a knock at his door broke across the quiet room. "Rob?" It was his mom. The door opened. "Are you all right?"

Rob raised himself onto an elbow. "Did anything come for me this afternoon?"

She shook her head. "I'm sorry."

"No big deal. He'll bring it when he comes. You know how busy Dad is."

"Rob"—she tried to smile—"I found this while I was cleaning your room."

She pulled a sheet of paper from beneath his notebook. "Will you please tell me what this note from Ms. Pickering is about?"

Rob's mind spun in circles, trying to invent an excuse.

"This note says that you have a number of incomplete assignments. Do you have them ready to hand in when you go back to school?"

Rob shook his head.

"Why not? You've had these last two weeks of vacation to catch up."

She moved closer. Her eyes, dark brown and searching, waited for his answer. But he didn't have an answer, at least not one she wanted to hear. She wanted him to be happy, happy like she was. "Put on a happy face for Mommy," was what she used to tell him just before dropping him off at the sitter's, then waving good-bye as she drove away to make her early-morning flight.

She sat next to him on the bed. Her perfume scented the air between them. "Rob," she said. One hand came up and brushed his cheek. "Are you unhappy because your father forgot to send you a Christmas gift?"

Rob glanced briefly at the photographs ringing his dresser mirror. Photographs of him and his dad. Finally, Rob shook his head. "Dad's really busy. He's always said that the end of the year is his busiest time. You remember."

He knew she remembered. He recognized that tight look. "Mom, it's okay that he forgot. I understand."

"Then what's wrong? Why are you falling behind in school?"

What's wrong? Did she really want to know? Or would she explain it away? *"Mommy has to leave but you're going to have a wonderful time here. I'll be home tomorrow evening. We'll pick your father up at his office and go out for pizza."* Then she would tuck her short, dark curls inside her airline cap.

He had hated the flight attendant's uniform that took her away every few days, the gray skin beneath her eyes when she returned, too tired to remember about stopping for his dad and going out for pizza.

"Rob!"

His mother never yelled. She whispered. His dad called it her "professional calm." But Rob knew when she meant business. He knew that she expected an answer . . . and *now*. She wanted to know what was wrong. She wanted his answer to be something she could reason away.

"It's this place," he finally said.

". . . this place? What's wrong with this place? Why are you having so many . . .?"

Problems was the word that hung between them. Rob knew he wasn't interested in school, knew he was an outsider among his classmates. "Seaweed from California" was what Brian Sass had called him.

She reached out, pressed her palm against his cheek. "You've always been a good student. I've never had to worry about you doing your homework. What's happened to change that?"

Her hand dropped back into her lap. "Is it Jim, my having remarried so—"

"No," he answered.

But it *was* Jim. It *was* her remarriage. It *was* this town. So why had he said no? Had he said no because he knew that was what she wanted to hear? "It's just me, I guess."

She said nothing for a long moment. Finally, "Well, I suggest you tell Mr. Me that he'd better get busy and have those assignments ready to hand in when he goes back to school Monday."

Wind out of the north drove against the house. A chill worked its way inside. "Mom, what am I going to do about Dad coming to visit?"

"What do you mean? You want to see him, don't you?"

"Sure, I really miss him but . . ."

"But what?"

Rob raised his leg, pointed to the swollen and discolored ankle. "Remember that time we were skiing at Mammoth?"

"Yes, and your father took a terrible risk skiing on a leg that might have been fractured."

"But he did it. He ignored the pain and did it."

"What is important to your father does not necessarily have to be important to you."

"But it is important to me."

"You have a severely sprained ankle. You can hardly walk."

Yeah, Rob thought. Coach Enge thinks so too. Says

I can't play hockey until next season. But Dad would compete; he'd find a way.

Shadows played across the ceiling, across his mother's pretty face as she backed to the door. "Can I count on you to get your homework done?"

Rob nodded. It was easy for her to say, "What is important to your father does not necessarily have to be important to you." She wasn't his son.

CHAPTER 3

Damp, gray mist hung above the lake and reached out toward town when Rob hobbled back upstairs after helping with the breakfast dishes. He pressed close to the window. Nothing moved beneath the frosty blanket. Rob shivered. The Polar Bears would be practicing, Coach Enge sending the squad through warm-up drills, Brian Sass blaming Rob, the California seaweed, for the team's only loss.

Brian Sass, book monitor in Rob's class, was boss of the lunchroom too. Rob blew his breath against the window, watched it fog the glass. Could his life get any worse? Yes, he supposed it could.

The sound of the garage door opening and a car's engine pulled Rob's gaze down between the two houses. He had promised his mother to have the math assignments completed by the time she and Jim returned for lunch. He wrote his name on the glass, then his dad's name before he sat down at the desk and flipped open the math book.

He hated math so he found himself sketching the *Sun Warrior* cutting through the swells off Point Loma, drew it resting on the beach in Coronado. Who cared what seven-eighths and three-fourths equaled? Rob wrote down one and five-eighths. By the time his mom and Jim arrived home from the festival-planning meeting and she called him to lunch, Rob had completed half of the math assignments and written his report on the exploration of the moon.

"That's wonderful," she said, and gave him a hug. "How's the ankle?"

"Great. I'll be walking good as new real soon."

"It looks terrible." Pointing to the empty chair beside Jim, she said, "Sit down and eat."

"Where's Doug?"

"Iceboating," Jim answered. "You ever been on an iceboat?"

"No, sir," Rob replied, and dipped his spoon into the bowl of chowder.

"There's a DN—a smaller-sized boat—in the boathouse. Hasn't been used since Doug was your age."

Jim Erikson coached football and baseball at Welholm Falls High School and taught history too. He told great stories about kayaking in Canada and the Iditarod. Rob knew he was there to listen to Doug when he needed to talk, and he showed up for all of Doug's games. Rob had no reason to dislike his new dad, yet he continued to call him sir, continued to be uneasy around him, continued to avoid being alone with him.

"It's great fun," Jim said. "Would you like to give it a try?"

Rob blew on the spoonful of soup. "Someday maybe."

After lunch Rob excused himself. But his mother asked Jim to look at his ankle, then insisted that it be wrapped. "To keep him from twisting it again," she said.

Doug returned home before the bandaging was completed. Cold reddened his cheeks. "It's fantastic out there," he said, and pulled the knitted face mask from over his head. "Boy, Dad, you got to see Mr. Enge's new boat. It's fast. Maybe the fastest Class A in the state."

Doug went on, pausing only to catch his breath. "He'll win this year's cup easy. No one in Welholm Falls has a boat that can even challenge his. You guys've got to see it."

When Jim finished wrapping Rob's ankle, he said, "How 'bout it, Rob? Want to ride in with your mom and me and have a look? We'll take the snowmobiles; cut across the lake."

Jim had broad shoulders and a smile to match. Rob had heard him yell, had seen him angry when fellows on the football team messed up. But now, Rob saw only kindness in Jim's blue eyes and a warmth that made Rob somehow uneasy. He turned aside, noticed his mom smiling, and knew she wanted him to come along. "Better not," Rob said. "I have to finish my homework."

Rob took little steps and tried not to limp until he

was upstairs and in his bedroom. He paused in front of the dresser to study the ring of photographs, to remember. But with all the good memories came a rush of bad ones—the continual fights between his parents, then the days of silence and how scared it made him feel. In some ways it was better living in Welholm Falls, except none of the guys liked him. At least Brian Sass didn't. Did a guy have to be perfect at everything to get others to like him? Rob turned to the window. The sun cracked open the sky. Made it a puzzle of blue and broken clouds. Everything else was white except for the sails that swept the iceboats over the lake—slashing splotches of brilliant reds, orange stripes, and blue.

Why had he refused Jim's invitation to ride to town to see Mr. Enge's boat? He liked riding on the snowmobile. Doug went over jumps and did really neat things. So why? Homework? He didn't think so.

He watched Jim and his mom climb onto one snowmobile, Doug onto the other. His mom had called her new husband a "warm and caring man, a secure man, a man who knows who he is."

Rob considered his mother's opinion of Jim. What did it mean to be secure, to know who you are? He knew his mother was happy. She laughed these days, her eyes no longer swollen and red. She held Jim's hand in the movies, sat close to him on the sofa. Sometimes Rob wondered why she had stopped loving his dad. He wondered if it was easy to stop loving someone. Sometimes it appeared to him that she loved Jim more than she loved him.

Rob fell across his bed. Sometimes he felt as if he had been dropped inside a giant mixer, his whole life, all of his feelings, everything he had ever counted on mixed up like scrambled eggs. He didn't want to live in Welholm Falls, didn't want a stepfather. He wanted to go home, back to everything being like it used to be. Even when they were fighting it was better than being a scrambled nothing, a piece of seaweed, that no one liked.

Rob's gaze followed the molding that separated ceiling from walls, while his thoughts dredged up images of his dad. A man who would demand to know why his son was a spectator instead of a participant . . . a man who was a winner.

His dad was vice president of a large company, piloted his own airplane, skied the expert slopes, and had a three handicap on the golf course. Larry Marshall was no loser, but Rob wondered about himself.

Rob raised his bad ankle, could almost hear his dad say, "Excuses are for losers."

He sat up, returned to the window. An iceboat, its sail dumped, rested alongside Jim's boathouse. Then Rob heard a banging on the back door. He hop-skipped across his room, rode the banister downstairs. "Sorry it took me so long," he said, recognizing Smitty behind the yellow visor and knitted face mask.

"Coach said one of us guys should come over and see how you're doing."

Smitty pulled the mask from over his eyes. "How's the ankle?"

"Great . . . no problem."

Smitty glanced down. "How come it's wrapped up?"

"My mom's idea. You know how scared they get."

Smitty nodded. "Freddie Markowski's got the chicken pox. C.J.'s gonna play goalie."

"You want to come in?"

"Can't." Smitty raised the legs of his insulated coveralls and displayed the ice creepers strapped to the bottoms of his boots.

"That your iceboat out back?" Rob asked.

"Yeah. It's a DN. Me and my dad built it, the *Windy Demon*."

"Is it hard to handle?"

"Naw." Smitty shot Rob a quick look. "You never been on an iceboat?"

"No. I'd sure like to give it a try. It looks like a lot of fun."

"You want to ride across the lake with me? I'll bring you back soon as I deliver my permission slip to the park's office. I got to turn this in before I can race the *Windy Demon* in the festival."

"I'll get my coat, okay?"

"Better cover up that foot, too. I'll wait outside."

It took Rob less than a minute to gather together parka, gloves, face mask, and extra socks. He wore one of Doug's boots on the sore foot and ran as best he could.

"How do you ride one of these things?" he yelled, and zipped the parka to his chin.

"Like it was a horse." Smitty pointed to a place behind the narrow cockpit. "I'll take it easy; nothing to get scared about. Just hang on to the backrest."

21

Rob threw his leg over the fuselage. "How long did it take you to learn how to pilot this?"

"Not long. Better keep your foot out of the way."

Smitty pushed the *Windy Demon* until the sail began to ripple and fill with wind, then he jumped into the cockpit.

The cold wind stung Rob's face, made his nose drip, his eyes water, and he wished for a helmet and face protector like the one Smitty wore. He knew, too, why Smitty wore insulated coveralls as the wind and all of its dampness cut through his jeans, sweater, and parka. "This is really great," he shouted. "Thanks for asking me along."

Rob paid close attention to how Smitty piloted the *Windy Demon*, how he held the tiller between his knees and used both hands to work the sheet. "This is a lot like maneuvering a windsurf," Rob said. "Why do you keep watching those ribbons tied to the bowstay?"

"That's the telltale and it tells me what the wind is doing."

It took only minutes to cross the lake and reach the park's office. Smitty set the parking brake. "If you should forget to set the brake and the wind catches the sail, you could end up chasing your boat across the lake."

Rob followed Smitty inside, opening his parka to the warmth. Posters covered every wall. Stacks of placards occupied each corner and a long table held ribbons that waited for team champions. Besides ribbons, engraved cups waited too, for the winners of the dog-sledding events, skijoring, snowmobile races, and trophies for the best-designed iceboat, the fastest, the most original.

When Smitty returned with his race permit, Rob asked, "If a guy was good at sailing, how long do you think it would take him to get the hang of iceboating?"

"Beats me." Smitty pulled on the face mask, his helmet, then adjusted the yellow visor over his eyes. "Someday, if you want, I'll let you have a shot at piloting mine."

"How about right now?"

"Can't. You need two good feet. Hang on."

Rob gripped the backrest with both hands as Smitty vaulted into the cockpit. Everyone at school called him Smitty except Ms. Pickering. She called him Frank. No one made jokes about his red hair, his freckled face, that he was short and round like a fireplug. And Smitty never made unkind remarks about anyone else. He wasn't best friends with Brian Sass the way Charlie Ellis was, but he wasn't Brian's enemy either. Smitty got along with everyone. He turned the *Windy Demon* into the wind, brought it around to a slow stop without using the hand brake.

"Thanks," Rob called, then stepped back and watched Smitty maneuver the *Windy Demon* out into the center of the lake. He made a sweeping turn, picked up the wind, pointed his craft toward town, toward the park's office, where all the ribbons and trophies waited for the winners.

CHAPTER 4

Rob asked a couple dozen questions at dinner about iceboats and participating in the Winter Festival Regatta. While his mother loaded the dishwasher, he continued to sit at the kitchen table with Jim and listened to Doug tell more about Mr. Enge's Class A, how fast it traveled, what the factory-built boat had cost. He talked until Jim said to Rob, "If you want to give iceboating a try, you're welcome to use the DN in the boathouse."

"Yeah!" Doug pushed back from the table. "I won fifth place with the *Snow Devil*. Remember, Dad?"

Fifth place hardly seemed like winning, Rob thought, as Doug went on talking. "I should have done better but it was my first year."

"And," Jim reminded, "there were only five boats in the amateur class race that year."

Doug grinned. "I was in the lead first time around, then I got cocky. I just knew I was going to walk away with the winner's trophy." He laughed. "But Mother Nature had other ideas. It was a real puffy day and we'd had a warming spell, so there were lots of waves out there."

"Waves," Jim explained, "are places of open water."

"I was having great fun riding two runners. Better than riding the roller coaster," Doug said. "But every time I crashed back onto the third runner, I lost a couple of seconds."

Rob had never talked to his own dad in the easy, good-natured way Doug talked to his dad. But Doug was older, maybe being older made a difference, allowed a son to talk to his dad like a best friend. "Did you build the *Snow Devil* yourself?" Rob asked.

"Well"—Doug grinned—"Dad did most of the work. He even taught me how to handle it. A few years back, he won the regatta three years running. No one else in Welholm Falls has ever done that."

Rob glanced in Jim's direction, expecting him to explain the difficulty of each race, how great his opponents had been, how long and hard he had prepared himself to be the winner the way his own dad would have done. But Jim sat quietly and drank his coffee.

"You ever been on an iceboat?" Doug asked.

Before Rob could tell him about crossing the lake on the *Windy Demon*, Doug laughed. "Not likely, coming from California. Stupid question."

Doug stood. "Come on," he said. "I've got a photo of the *Snow Devil* in my bedroom."

Rob was already out of the chair before he asked to be

excused. He hurried after Doug, followed him upstairs. While Doug rummaged through one dresser drawer after another, Rob examined the row of trophies—hockey, tennis, wrestling. "A DN like the one Dad and I built can be a lot of fun," Doug said. "They don't travel the speeds that the big ones do, but they go fast enough."

"Can anyone enter the festival races?"

"Sure; they have all divisions." Doug offered the photograph. "The *Snow Devil* didn't please the old eyeballs the way the factory-built boats do today, but she sure could hike. Not only is it like riding a roller coaster sideways, you're less than two feet off the surface of the ice and sometimes hitting speeds above fifty miles an hour. It can get real scary, but the sensation is like nothing you've ever felt before."

Rob bit his lower lip. "Are they hard to maneuver?"

"You don't maneuver an iceboat, you pilot the baby and once you get the hang of how the tiller controls the front steering runner and how to tack, you've got it made."

"That's all there is to it?"

"Mostly. When your ankle heals, you can take the *Snow Devil* out, see for yourself how easy she is to handle. I know Dad will help out. He's a great teacher, taught me all that I know."

Doug took back the picture. "With all the windsurfing you did in California, you should be a surefire cinch."

"No kidding?"

"No kidding." Doug unbuttoned his shirt collar.

"The *Snow Devil* is down in the boathouse. Take it out whenever you like."

"Tomorrow?"

Doug laughed. "Not likely. You need two good feet."

"My ankle's okay. Watch." Rob crossed the room, taking his time, limping only slightly.

"Tell you what," Doug said. "Whenever your mom gives the okay, you can take it out. And if Dad isn't around, I'll give you a couple of pointers, if you want."

Rob's nod was less than enthusiastic. He knew his mother would have other ideas. But he hadn't counted on her having so many objections.

First there were gale winds blowing and below-zero temperatures. "A person could get frostbite out there," she said.

When he asked again, she pointed to his ankle and said, "It's still twice its normal size. I don't want you out on that ice until your ankle heals."

Just before leaving for school Monday morning, he asked again for permission to take the *Snow Devil* out for a trial run later in the afternoon. "No," she said. "You'll just have to wait. Learning to pilot that boat isn't a life-or-death matter."

But it was. She knew his dad was coming. She knew the importance he placed on winning. And Rob knew he could be a winner if only he had enough time.

CHAPTER 5

Rob thought about skipping school after he left home Monday morning. He thought about it again when the long building and flagpole were in sight. He needed all the time he could get in the *Snow Devil*. And it was a great day for being on the lake. No wind, plenty of sunshine, and his ankle felt better, even though it continued to look fat. But skipping school in Welholm Falls wasn't the same as skipping school in San Diego. Ms. Pickering would turn it into a criminal case, call his mother and everything. His mom just might ground him too, ground him until after Winter Festival and his dad's visit. So Rob decided against skipping school. He had to stay cool. Do what was expected. He spent the morning thinking about his dad's visit. He heard himself talking to his dad about iceboating in the same relaxed way Doug talked to Jim. Was he old enough to talk to his dad that way? Would his dad stand for it? While the other boys in Rob's class shared lunch, Rob ate alone. He didn't mind. He had a lot going on in his mind. Rob spent the afternoon watching the clock, counting the minutes, groaning inwardly when Ms. Pickering added another page of numbers to the blackboard. No doubt about it, she wanted every minute of his free time:

FOUR PAGES OF MATH; READ PAGES 144 THROUGH 157 AND BE PREPARED FOR A QUIZ ON THE LOUISIANA PURCHASE; WRITE A FOURTEEN-LINE POEM BEST DESCRIBING YOUR FEELINGS ABOUT WINTER FESTIVAL.

The afternoon bell rang in Rob's ears, but Ms. Pickering motioned everyone back to their places. "As you know, the city gives an award each year to the person contributing the best original piece of art depicting Winter Festival. This year," she went on, "I want each of you to take an active part. I'm making it an assignment."

Rob inched toward the edge of his seat. Okay, he thought, it turns dark at five and I don't know the first thing about getting an iceboat onto the ice.

"Rob Marshall," Ms. Pickering said, "please remain. The rest of you are dismissed."

Rob sank back. Too late, he thought, and scowled at his classmates as they filed from the room. *Turtles move faster.*

Rob watched his teacher from the corner of his eye as she leafed through the assignments he had spent the last few days of vacation doing. When the door finally swung shut and they were alone, she said, "Is this hon-

29

estly the best work you're capable of doing? Come up here."

Was she going to make him do it over?

"Look at this." She pushed a paper at him. "This is the poorest science report I've seen all year. A half page. Couldn't you find more to say about the exploration of the moon than eighteen lines?"

Rob saw her eyes studying him. Unable to decide what she was going to do, Rob looked aside.

"Look at me when I'm speaking to you," she said.

He raised his head. She went on: "Where is your book report? It was due today."

"I didn't finish it."

"When will you have it ready to hand in?"

He shrugged.

"Have you finished reading your book?"

"No, ma'am." He tried to swallow, but his throat was too dry. "I haven't decided on a book that I want to read."

"You mean you haven't even *selected* a book?"

Ms. Pickering sank into her chair. She waited, then spoke with a softer tone. "I realize you've had some changes in your life, but I don't have the feeling you're trying to help yourself."

But I am, he wanted to tell her: I want to learn to pilot the *Snow Devil* and win a trophy. I want to make my dad really proud of me. Rob said, "Yes, ma'am."

"Is there anything you would like to talk over with me? I'm very good at listening, even better at keeping secrets."

She smiled. She was pretty, he thought, but not

beautiful like his mother. He wondered if telling her about his dad visiting Welholm Falls for Festival Weekend would get her off his back. Probably not. The only things teachers cared about were if a fellow could see the blackboard and hear the assignments.

Ms. Pickering grew tired of waiting, leaned back in her chair. "Unless you prove to me, during the next four weeks, that you can do the work and are handing in the assignments on time, I'll have to give you an incomplete on your grade card."

Rob blinked. *Incomplete on my grade card?* He tried to swallow.

"And," she went on, "before I do that, I'll call in your parents for a conference."

"Don't do that. I'll do better. I promise."

She waited and watched. "I'll give you a couple of weeks to catch up, but if I don't see a big improvement—"

"You will," Rob interrupted. "You won't have to call my mom."

She stood. "The downtown library is open until nine o'clock. I suggest you select a book and report the title and author to me first thing tomorrow."

"Yes, ma'am."

She returned the science report. "I'll accept the math papers even though they are poorly done, but I want at least a two-page report on some phase of moon exploration."

Rob nodded. He backed from the room. "Holy somoley," he whispered, aware that he had missed a complete disaster by a skinny inch. He zipped his parka, pulled the red stocking cap over his ears, then rushed to the end of the hall where Jennifer waited.

Her blond hair stuck out beneath her pink stocking cap. She looked at Rob with her blue eyes and asked, "Did you get into trouble?"

Rob led the way outside. Brian, Charlie Ellis, and Jerry Canady huddled together near the flagpole. They kept looking over their shoulders as Rob and Jennifer passed, muttering, snickering. Rob's fingers drew up into tight knots. One day, he promised himself, one day.

"Rob," Jennifer asked, "did you get into trouble?"

"Not me."

"Where are you going?"

"To the library."

"Library? The book report!" Jennifer whispered as if she had found a dollar bill. "I made my report on Mozart. It was a biography. I've read about Brahms, Bach, and Beethoven. Do you know who those men were?"

Of course he knew. He knew why Jennifer read books about the lives of composers too. She took piano lessons every Saturday morning. His mom said Jennifer was gifted.

"Hey, you guys," Smitty called. "Wait up."

"Rob's going to the library," Jennifer said. "He hasn't made his book report and Ms. Pickering is mad."

"I got my report in on time," Smitty said. "My dad has this really great book about Mickey Thompson. He set a world's speed record at the Bonneville Salt Flats in Utah."

They stopped at the corner. Waving, Jennifer turned for home while Rob and Smitty crossed the boulevard. Smitty shifted his books to the other arm. "I'm taking the *Windy Demon* out this afternoon if you want to come along."

"I'd really like to," Rob said, "but Ms. Pickering said if I didn't get my book report turned in, she'd give me an incomplete." Rob matched his stride to Smitty's. "How long have you had the *Windy Demon?*"

"Couple of years. But my dad's been teaching me about piloting a boat since I was eight."

"And you won first place last year?"

"Yeah, I beat Brian by a couple of minutes, but it won't be so easy this year. His grandmother bought him a new DN, factory-built. It's really slick."

Smitty stopped at the corner of Fourth and Lakefront. "See you," he said, and bent his head against the wind and continued up the street while Rob headed for the library.

He thought about Brian and his factory-built DN. Could he beat him and his new boat with only a few weeks' experience? Rob broke into a limp-run and covered the four blocks in half the normal time.

The library felt warm. The floors creaked beneath his weight, and the silence smelled of paper and floor wax. Jennifer's mom stood behind the checkout desk and waved as Rob threw his coat over the back of a chair. "Hi," he whispered. "I have to make a book report. Can you help me find a skinny book?"

She led Rob to a shelf of paperbacks. "This is a very

good one. It's about a boy who goes off to live on a mountain by himself."

The idea sounded neat, but the book was too fat. He needed something he could read really quickly. Maybe he should report on one of the books he had read last year in San Diego; Ms. Pickering would never know the difference. But Rob continued to look. Instead of finding thinner volumes, they grew thicker, the titles weirder. Why would he want to make a report on basket weaving or basset hounds, Mozart or Mickey Thompson? Beavers and beetles failed to interest him, too. Then, Rob stopped. *Boating: From Canoes to Yachts. Boat Plans for the Home Craftsman. Boating for All Ages.*

Rob jerked the last book from the shelf and hurried with it to a table. Iceboats began on page 278. Diagrams . . . pictures . . . instructions. A glossy-colored print stretched across two pages. The sail looked larger than a circus tent. Rob flipped from one page to the next, looking for something smaller, something called a DN. Page 291 was subtitled Iceboating for the Beginner.

Rob leaned closer: "Iceboats are alive. They respond to the slightest touch. On the ice, the speed, the sounds, and the wind leave one with the feeling of flying in an open-cockpit airplane."

Rob whistled softly: "It is advisable for the inexperienced pilot to spend at least one winter helping friends with their boats. The beginner who jumps into an iceboat is like a person taking off in a single-seat airplane without previous training. As there is more to flying than handling the stick, there is more to iceboating than working the sheet."

Rob sat straight. A whole year? A year was too long. What had Doug said? "With all the windsurfing you did in California, you should be a surefire cinch."

Rob slammed the book shut. Book writers weren't authorities; they could be wrong. Doug knew about everything; he'd learned it from his dad. Rob reopened the book. At the end of the chapter was a list of references. Rob ran his finger down the titles. He stopped. *The Art of Sailing All Types of Boats.*

Rob hurried back to the bookshelf. He found it on the bottom row. He opened it and read as he carried it back to the table: "The man or woman who comes into iceboating with previous skills in sailing normally has little trouble making the change to iceboating."

"Yeah!" He went on flipping from page to page. There were photographs, step-by-step instructions on how to pilot an iceboat.

"Rob." Ms. Johannsen spoke again. "Rob, do you realize it's nearly six. Won't your mother be—"

Rob jumped up.

Ms. Johannsen took the book. Her lips moved with the title, then her gaze shifted to Rob. "You're going to report on this book?"

"You bet. I can do a really terrific report. It's loaded with great stuff."

As she prepared to check out the book, she asked, "Are you thinking of a sailboat for summer or an iceboat?"

"First thing I have to do is turn in a book report, then—"

"Suppose we talk about it on the walk home," she said. "I'd enjoy your company."

Rob began telling her about Doug's DN and how he would like to race it in the festival regatta while she slipped into her coat, wrapped a scarf over her head, and put on fleecy gloves.

"Do you know anything about iceboating?" she asked.

Rob pointed to the book. "Doug told me too, that if a guy can handle a windsurf, then it's a breeze. And I had my own windsurf when I lived in California. I was really good at it."

"I'm sure you were and I don't mean to disagree with your brother, but there's much more to iceboating than meets the eye. Your stepfather spent years learning to be a good and safe pilot."

The cold air stung Rob's cheeks and forced him to zip up his parka to the throat, pull the hood over his head. He followed Ms. Johannsen around the corner and through the park. He knew he could learn enough in these next few weeks to be a winner.

They stopped in front of the Johannsens' driveway. Jennifer's mother smiled. "You had better hurry along if you plan to finish that book this evening."

"You're right. See you, Ms. Johannsen." Rob drew his shoulders up around his ears. He waited until she stepped inside her house before he spun around on his good foot.

Doug had said he was a cinch; the author of the book he carried under his arm said so too. Sometimes women just didn't understand about how fast a guy could learn something that was really important. With Doug teaching him, he would beat Brian even if Sass did have a new boat. He'd beat Smitty too but knew that would be more difficult.

He envisioned his dad's face as he, Rob Marshall, walked up to the presenters' table and accepted the winner's trophy. Rob smiled.

CHAPTER 6

Rob set aside his dream of winning a trophy, rewrote the science paper, and completed the new math assignments. He stayed up past ten and finished the book report. When he laid them on Ms. Pickering's desk the next morning, she frowned. Rob guessed at her thought—*another lousy job.*

That afternoon, just before the final bell, she returned his papers. The science report had an okay, while there were penciled comments on the back of the book report: "This is good work. It shows some thought and enthusiasm. It's not the kind of book I would pick to review, but I can understand why you might. I liked your comparison of iceboating to open-cockpit flying. Do I take it from this report that you'll be entering an iceboat in the Winter Festival competition?"

After class was dismissed, Rob hurried into the hallway. He pulled Jennifer away from her friends. "Rob Marshall," she exclaimed, "let go of me."

"I have to talk to you." He looked in all directions. "I need your help. We have to hurry too."

Once outside, Jennifer stopped. "It's freezing," she said, and buttoned her coat against the wind.

Rob jerked on her arm. "Come on. We have to hurry!"

"Where are we going?"

"I can't tell you. It's a secret."

"Secret?" Jennifer hurried to keep up with Rob's jerking stride. "What's the secret? Are you going to flunk or what?"

"Not hardly. Let's hurry."

Though his ankle began to ache and worsened his limp, he kept several steps ahead of Jennifer. Winter days were short, afternoon temperatures dropped rapidly, and he had homework. "Come on, Jennifer. Hurry."

Rob was puffing and out of breath when he reached home. He danced around on one foot, swung his arms to keep warm until Jennifer reached hearing distance. "Change into warm clothes," he called to her. "Then meet me at my boathouse. I've got something really fantastic to show you."

"I'm not going to meet you anyplace unless you tell me your secret. It's freezing. It's going to snow."

"If you want to know my secret, meet me at the boathouse. And it's not going to snow!"

His mother was on the telephone when he hurried through the kitchen, but he left the book report with Ms. Pickering's comments on the table for her to see. He changed into warmer clothes, put on extra socks before slipping into Doug's insulated coveralls.

He grabbed the library book from his desk and hurried downstairs. His mother, still on the phone, flashed him a smile, pointed an approving finger at Ms. Pickering's note. Rob grabbed paper and pencil.

"Mom," he wrote, "gone iceboating with Jennifer."

Then he ran outside, the library book tucked beneath his arm. Cold air, like a thick white wall, hit him. He caught his breath, felt the chill all the way into his lungs. Crazy, that's what he was, crazy! But Rob kept running until he reached the boathouse. He unlatched the wide double doors and pulled the *Snow Devil* onto the ice.

When Jennifer arrived, she said, "Tell me the secret, Rob Marshall, or I'm going home this minute."

Rob pointed to the *Snow Devil*. "Doug said I could take it out for a trial run."

"That's your secret?"

"Yeah. I'm going to sign up for the festival regatta. I'm gonna win too."

"Rob Marshall, it's twelve below zero out here."

"So it's a little cold. You'll warm up. Give me a hand."

It was obvious that Jennifer didn't want to help. Her blue eyes sparked. She complained continually about the cold and his lack of good sense. Sure, he would have preferred being indoors, drinking hot chocolate and playing video games. But time was short. He had to practice every day until Festival Weekend, no matter how low the temperatures dropped. A guy couldn't expect to win unless he practiced. His dad was proof of that, and Rob was going to be a winner just like his dad.

He raised the mast, locked it into position. He noticed the tattered telltale and the way the wind whipped it about the bowstay, the blue-black sky off to the north. "Grab hold of the halyard," he yelled.

"What's the halyard?"

"That line right in front of you. Pull it to raise the sail." Rob hurried to the other side of the boat. "Okay, haul."

Jennifer glanced around.

"Haul!" Rob yelled.

"Haul what?"

"Jennifer," he shouted, "haul means to pull. If your dad is into iceboats, how come you don't know anything about them?"

Jennifer stomped her foot. "It's freezing out here and I don't have to know anything about iceboats if I don't want to."

He felt the wind, the frigid air work their way through his many layers of clothing. He shivered, as the wall of blue-black sky moved closer. "Will you please haul? I mean, pull."

The sail crept upward, but as it did, Rob counted four holes the size of golf balls. "Shoot!" Rob shouted, and pointed to the holes. "That sail won't hold a speck of wind."

Jennifer stepped closer, studied the holes as if she had an idea. "Iron-on patches will work. Mother has a package of them."

"You're terrific. We'll need an iron too."

Jennifer hesitated. Rob saw her shoulders stiffen.

41

"Please," he said, "you're the only one I can count on to help me."

After a moment, Jennifer ran to her house. Rob took in the sail. When she returned, she handed him the scissors and plugged in the iron. Rob cut and shaped each patch, then impatiently waited while Jennifer ironed them to the sail. "If we hurry," he said, "we can get rigged and still have forty minutes of daylight."

"It's nearly dark now."

The rigging took five extra minutes.

"Rob," Jennifer protested, "it's going to snow, and the way the wind is blowing—"

"You sit back here."

"Back where?"

"Here behind the cockpit."

"It's all splintery. I'll ruin my new pants. Don't you know that it's real easy to get frostbite in weather like this?"

Rob ignored Jennifer's warnings. He ignored the cold working its way through his skin, chilling his blood. "Hang on to the backrest," he told her. "And if you sit really still, you won't tear your pants. Okay?"

But Jennifer didn't answer. "Once I get us started," he explained, "I'll jump inside the cockpit. Okay?"

"How will you do that with a sore ankle?"

"My ankle's okay."

Jennifer gave Rob a side glance that questioned his good sense before she threw her leg over the fuselage and sat down carefully. Then he handed her the library book, open to the step-by-step set of instructions.

"What am I supposed to do—read this to you?"

"You catch on quick. Read loud, okay."

"Rob!"

The iceboat started forward, and Jennifer moaned. The sail shook and filled with wind. Rob pushed faster, felt the muscles in his ankle tighten and sting. Suddenly his ankle twisted. He went down onto his knees, but he refused to release the runner plank.

"Jennifer," he shouted as the *Snow Devil* picked up speed.

"Rob? Rob, we're going too fast. Stop this thing right now!"

The *Snow Devil* went faster, pulled him through shallow drifts and over lumpy ice. "Dump the wind, Jennifer! Pull the sheet. That rope in front of the cockpit—pull it!"

Jennifer's arm shot across the empty cockpit. She jerked hard. The sail came about, and the *Snow Devil* began to slow. "More muscle," Rob shouted. "Put more muscle into it."

Jennifer used both hands. The iceboat swung around, stopped.

Slowly Rob pulled up. His ankle throbbed, felt broken though he knew it wasn't, and he knew that if he started limping again, his mother would ground him. Rob brushed the snow away, cleaned his goggles. "Let's try it again."

"Again?"

"I'm not a quitter. Again!" Rob slid down inside the cockpit. "I wouldn't have fallen down if I'd had a set of ice creepers on the bottoms of my boots. We'll go out just a little farther, then head back, okay?"

"No, it's not okay. Turn this thing around right now."

"Just a little farther," he coaxed. "I'll be really careful."

"We could catch pneumonia out here and be dead in the morning."

"Hang on to the backrest," he told her, and shrugged her hands from his shoulders.

Rob adjusted the sail. The canvas rippled, but the *Snow Devil* refused to budge. Rob moved the tiller right, then left. "Bounce," Rob shouted, while lifting his weight up and down.

Finally the runners broke free. The sail filled with wind. "Read, Jennifer. Read loud."

Her voice wavered. " 'There are two ways to control the speed of the iceboat: ease off on the sheet or turn closer into the wind.' "

The *Snow Devil* swung left. Rob cranked the tiller windward. The boat slowed. "How about that! Read more, Jennifer."

" 'To increase the speed,' " she continued, " 'turn the steering runner off the wind and expose much of the sail's surface to the wind source.' "

Rob followed the book's directions before he glanced up at the telltale. Just as the *Snow Devil* shot ahead, he realized that his angle was wrong. The windward runner lifted and tilted the boat.

Jennifer screamed. She grabbed Rob around the neck. He tried to work the sheet with one hand and pull her fingers from around his throat with the other. "Jennifer," he gasped, "let go."

Rob cranked the tiller starboard and dumped the sail. The *Snow Devil* swung about like the last man on a crack-the-whip. Jennifer jumped free of the fuselage, threw the library book into the cockpit alongside Rob. "You nearly killed us," she shouted.

"And you nearly strangled me." Rob pulled free of the cockpit. "Jennifer? Hey, where are you going?"

Rob hop-skipped to catch up. "Come on," he called. "I've got the hang of it now."

She walked faster.

"I won't scare you anymore. I promise."

But she lowered her head against the wind and continued walking. "Okay," Rob called out, "go home. See if I care. See if I ever share any more secrets with you."

As Rob swung around, he saw the *Snow Devil* creep away. Slowly at first, but as the wind brought the sail about, the boat picked up speed. The brake! He'd forgotten to set the brake.

He couldn't let the *Snow Devil* get away, end up a wreck on the far side of the lake. Rob forced his legs faster until he caught hold of the backrest with one hand, the sheet with the other.

". . . there's much more to iceboating than meets the eye," Jennifer's mother had said. But Rob knew about the parking brake. Just because he had forgotten to do a simple thing didn't mean it was going to take him a *year* to learn.

Rob secured the library book inside the cockpit. He

checked the telltale's position to the hull, eased out on the sheet, then began a stiff-legged sort of limp-run, and pushed against the runner plank until the wind took control. Rob vaulted into the cockpit, grimaced as the pain in his ankle ripped through every part of his body.

The *Snow Devil* glided ahead in a leeward direction, carried him farther out toward the center of the lake, then beyond toward the blue-black curtain. Rob sighed—a slow, soft kind of sound that accompanied the sense of relief that momentarily pushed aside the cold.

Rob studied the telltale, then adjusted the sheet and tiller as the wind shifted direction. He brought the boat about, pointed the steering runner to the south and the vague outlines of houses behind the thickening gray of early evening.

Rob eased back, relaxed his grip. He heard the wind, the *swoosh* of the runner blades, the rippling canvas. But it was the frigid cold that Rob noticed the most.

He felt it through layers of clothing, through his skin, deep inside his bones. It numbed his fingers, stiffened his limbs, worked up to his brain, and infected his mind. Occupied it with the same dullness that seized nerves and muscles, blocked every mental impulse. Nothing was easy. It took effort and concentrated thought to work the tiller, handle the sheet. Only when the boat began to behave strangely did he remember to look up and check the telltale.

The misalignment sent a wave of panic careening through him. Doubt and fear grabbed him and tried to take charge. It took every bit of Rob's determination to snatch back control from a mind and body that had slowed to half speed, from the gripping cold that settled slowly over the lake.

Each time Rob read the telltale, realized that he needed to readjust the sheet, a slow, step-by-step and deliberate process began. There were no instinctive reactions now. It took seconds before the thought became the act.

Trees and houses, smoke curling out of chimneys, and other iceboats suddenly snapped into focus. What had looked to be a long way off was suddenly before him.

Nothing in windsurfing had prepared him for iceboating—the speed, the wind, the cold, his inability to judge distances, to think, to remember. . . .

". . . there's much more to iceboating than meets the eye."

Rob understood about tacking, understood about keeping his boat at right angles with the wind. He was confident that once he closed in on the other boats he could maneuver the *Snow Devil* to the boathouse without any problems.

Letting out the sheet acted as a brake. He made similar adjustments with the tiller that kept the steering runner pointed toward home. Rob practiced the maneuver over and over until he did it smoothly. And his confidence grew.

The *Snow Devil* picked up speed—twenty, maybe twenty-five. The *swoosh* of the honed runners skimming over the ice made him shiver. He recognized Smitty's *Windy Demon*, Brian's new DN, and he moved in closer to show them both that there was something he could do as well as either of them.

Rob heard the sail rattle, looked up at the telltale, but it was already too late. The *Snow Devil* heeled over, skimmed the bumpy surface on two runners, hurtled down on the slower moving boats directly ahead.

Rob's knees froze against the tiller. Bumps on the ice caused the steering runner to vibrate. The tiller wrenched back and forth—left, then right. The *Snow Devil* shook violently.

Rob slid forward, then off to one side as the *Snow Devil* crashed back onto its third runner, whipped around, whipped around a second time. Stopped dead.

Other iceboats closed in. "Hey," Smitty shouted, "I thought you didn't know about iceboating. That was one scary maneuver."

"Stupid!" Brian shouted, and jumped free of the new fiberglass fuselage of his factory-built DN. Its new sail looked like freshly hung laundry. Rob envied him the boat but not the reasons for his having it. Everyone in Welholm Falls knew that Brian's grandmother spoiled him with expensive gifts to make up for his mother running off. And Brian knew that everyone in town knew about his mom. Painted along the bow of Brian's new boat was the name *Annihilator*.

"You ever come crashing in on me like that again with that piece of junk and I'll personally dent your gourd beyond repair."

"Reverse the rattle," Smitty yelled, and pulled out of his cockpit. "Rob didn't come within fifty feet of your boat."

"Says who?"

"Me, that's who." Smitty turned his back. "You handle that thing better than I ever thought you would. Either you were lucky or you're a pretty fair pilot." Smitty pushed his helmet to the back of his head. "I figure you were five seconds away from a high-speed capsize."

"Everything happened so fast, and the cold—"

"Yeah," Smitty said, "it slows down a guy's reaction time."

"There's more to this than I thought," Rob said. "It's like windsurfing but it's not."

Smitty gave the *Snow Devil* a push.

"See you tomorrow," Rob called, and pointed the steering runner toward home.

Would there be enough time to make himself into a winning pilot? Did the *Snow Devil* have one last race in it, or was it just a piece of junk as Brian said?

CHAPTER 7

After dinner Rob told his mother he would wait for Doug in the boathouse. "He's going to give me some pointers about racing."

Rob ran from the house, ran the short distance, and let himself in. He found the light switch nearby. He closed the door, shut out the cold and the droning wind as it whipped across the lake. It was warmer inside but still cold. He saw his breath, gray in the pale overhead light. Would it be snowing before morning, stopping him from getting in another day of practice?

Shadows fell around the iceboat. Rob stepped closer. Brian's voice rang in his ears: " . . . that piece of junk." Was the *Snow Devil* junk, or was it Brian's new boat that made every other boat appear to be junk?

Rob circled the *Snow Devil*. The runners were dull and rusty. The chocks that held them to the runner plank were rusty. The paint on the fuselage was cracked, peeling in places, splintery in other places. Iron-on patches dotted the sail. The varnished mast was yellowed and checked. The pulleys needed lubricating.

Just junk?

Could it be repaired?

How had he missed seeing all of its flaws? Why had it taken Brian's criticism to open his eyes to the *Snow Devil*'s imperfections? Rob circled the boat several more times. "I'm gonna fix you up," Rob whispered. "I'll ask Smitty. Doug will tell me what needs to be done too."

The plywood deck needed to be reglued and repainted, the chock fittings cleaned, the runners sharpened. And Rob thought about Brian's *Annihilator*, its red, fiberglass hull, the white sail, the factory-sharpened runners.

Sure, it would be a great advantage to have a new boat. With a new boat . . . Man, he could win easy!

Rob took a ladder from against the wall, opened it, set it next to the boat, then climbed to the top to examine the sail and the many tiny holes he had missed seeing earlier.

His mom had a sewing machine; she made everything. Could she make him a new sail? Would she? Sitting on the top of the ladder and letting his legs dangle over the side, Rob tried to honestly evaluate the *Snow Devil*. The longer he thought about all the things that would have to be repaired, the closer he came to crying.

The outer door opened. Cold air and whistling wind followed Jim inside. He closed the door. "Your mother said you were down here waiting for Doug. He just called. He'll be late getting home. Anything I can do?"

Rob shook his head, but Jim stepped closer. "How do things look from up there?"

"Not so good."

Jim ran his hand along the fuselage. "Your mother said that you took it out this afternoon. How did it go?"

"I got us both back in one piece."

Jim bent down, tested the steering runner's sharpness with his thumb. Rob started to explain that the runner had been nicked before he took it out, but Jim said, "This may have caused you some trouble, definitely slowed you down. But it's easily fixed."

Jim backed away, studied the *Snow Devil*, then laughed. "It looks like a pile of junk," he said, and laughed again. "If you're thinking that you'd like to pilot this iceboat, you have some work to do."

And Jim began to name off the repairs that needed to be made. He asked Rob again how his first ride had gone. This time, Rob tried to explain every detail, how the boat had acted and responded, how it felt to be out there less than two feet above the surface of the ice, going faster than the wind, being totally responsible for what happened to himself and the boat. "It was real scary at times. The cold was awful."

"You have to respect the cold; it's nothing to fool with," Jim said, and nodded as if he knew. "The first thing that you need to do is get the proper clothes. You'll need a helmet, insulated boots, and ice creepers to strap to the bottoms of your boots."

Jim smiled. He reached up and rested a hand on Rob's knee. "It took a lot of determination to go out there this afternoon all by yourself and do what you did."

"I wasn't exactly alone," Rob admitted. "Jennifer went with me, then the windward runner lifted off the ice, and she got scared." Rob hesitated, considered. "It scared me too. Once I got the *Snow Devil* stopped, Jennifer hopped off and wouldn't get back on. She's really mad at me."

"Maybe it would make her less angry if you told her that you'd been scared too. And if she understood why competing in the regatta is so important to you . . . it is important to you, isn't it?"

"Yes, sir. I have to make . . ." Rob stopped. The intensity in Jim's blue eyes forced Rob to consider whether or not he wanted to explain to a stranger why being the kind of son his dad expected was so important. "Yes, sir," Rob repeated. "I really do want to do this."

Jim withdrew his hand from around Rob's knee, circled the *Snow Devil.* "If you had the time, I know you'd like to take on the repair of this boat yourself. Since your time is so short, would you like me to give you a hand?"

Rob's mouth dropped open. "You mean it?"

"I don't want to interfere if you've made other arrangements."

"No, sir. I'd be really grateful for your help." Rob chewed on his bottom lip before he said, "Fact is, I've never built or fixed anything except for changing a tire on my bike. My dad always . . ."

Again, Rob stopped short. He felt the silence between them and all of its awkwardness. It pressed him to continue; Jim waited. Rob jumped down from the ladder, stood next to Jim to avoid his eyes. "Since I don't know all the things that need fixing, if you'll just tell me and show me how, I'll do the work."

"You've got courage," Jim said, and ruffled Rob's hair. "Besides there being a lot of work here, learning to be a good pilot is no easy thing, no matter how much sailing experience you've had."

Rob slid his shoe across the gritty floor. He could do it; he knew he could. He said, "I know how to use a screwdriver and push sandpaper. I can start smoothing out those bad spots on the fuselage right now."

"Why don't we go back to the house where it's warm and make up a list of the things that need repairing or replacing? I'll need to get some wood down here for the stove too."

Rob followed Jim to the door. "Mom sews really well. I'll bet she can make me a new sail. I've got about forty-eight dollars saved up. That ought to pay for the cloth, don't you think?"

Jim snapped off the light. "It might cost a bit more than forty-eight dollars."

When they reached the house, Jim added, "Suppose you could go into town tomorrow afternoon and speak to Harry Enge about a new runner plank? You'll need a good piece of laminated spruce with some spring in it. Think you can do that?"

"You bet," Rob answered. "Just as soon as school's out. Maybe I can even talk Jennifer into going with me."

CHAPTER 8

The following morning, Rob hurried from the house, along with his books and Jim's list. He stopped off for Jennifer, intending to admit that yesterday's ride had scared him too. But Jennifer had left earlier. Rob walked the six blocks alone. Besides the usual silence from Brian, Canady, and Ellis, Jennifer ignored him too.

Rob ate lunch in the farthest back corner of the cafeteria while Jennifer sat with her girlfriends and giggled. Smitty had lunchroom duty and there were Brian, Canady, Ellis. . . . Rob pushed his lunch tray aside, watching Brian. He acted like he was king of the world.

But one day last summer, Brian had been less than king. Rob remembered seeing him and his buddies at the community pool. Brian had just done a belly flop off the high board. Everyone gave him the horse laugh. Rob remembered laughing too, remembered taking his turn off the high board and doing a perfect half-gainer that made Jennifer cheer. No one else said anything.

A couple of weeks later school started and Brian began calling him "Seaweed." When hockey practice started, Brian went out of his way to prove to everyone that the newcomer from California had shoelaces for ankles, raisins for brains, and was unworthy of wearing a Polar Bears' uniform.

It seemed to Rob as he watched Sass, Ellis, and Canady that to be accepted in Welholm Falls, you first had to be accepted by Brian Sass, who thought he had to be the best at everything.

As soon as school was dismissed, Rob hurried from the building. He followed Lakefront, then cut across the end of the lake to the park's office. He asked for the permission slip that would allow him to compete, and was told that before he could be assigned a number for the regatta, he would have to bring in his boat for inspection.

Rob skip-hopped along the downtown streets, past storefronts, past the endless line of leafless trees that bordered the sidewalk. A few blocks later he slowed to a walk as he saw A–Z Salvage, a converted dairy barn and ten-acre junkyard. Sunlight caught on the shiny fuselage of a World War II navy trainer and bounced off. Alongside crates of landing gears rested piles of camouflaged wing tanks and ammunition boxes.

Rob hurried inside. Voices ricocheted off ceiling-high racks of surplus military gear, parachutes, and clothing. Rob stopped long enough to admire a Red Baron flying cap.

"Rob . . ."

The voice sounded familiar. "Rob, is that you?"

"Hi, Mr. Enge." Rob dug into his pocket for Jim's list. He presented it with pride and the satisfaction of knowing he had helped compile it.

Mr. Enge's eyes jumped from line to line. "Are you and Jim going to build a new boat or repair an old one?"

"We're gonna fix up the *Snow Devil*. I took it out yesterday."

Rob felt the permissions slip inside his pocket. "Doug says that I'm a natural because I've had a lot of experience with windsurfs. Sailboats too."

Rob caught the older man's side glance. "I don't mean to discourage you from competing, but you'll need more than windsurf experience to race against the boys in your age group. Frank Smith was last year's winner and Brian Sass has a new factory-built DN. Then, there are boys with good boats from the neighboring towns." Mr. Enge raised a hand to Rob's shoulder. "Competition will be tough. Is Jim going to teach you to pilot the *Snow Devil*?"

"Smitty and Doug have offered to help. I took it out yesterday by myself."

"That's fine, but if you want to give your friends a race, you'll ask Jim for his help. There's not much that he doesn't know about getting a DN through a racecourse in record time."

Mr. Enge motioned for Rob to follow. "The *Snow Devil* was a fine craft when Jim built it. Doug might have won, had he been patient and known more about tacking. That's not something you can learn in a couple of weeks. Not even a racing season."

Rob's voice rose to a higher pitch. "But I know about tacking. I'm really good at it too."

57

Mr. Enge opened the side door, turned on the light. "That's *Winter Storm*, she's my Class A."

The boat that Doug said no one in Welholm Falls could even begin to challenge. Rob walked the length of the sleek, fiberglass fuselage—aluminum boom, brass fittings. "She's a beauty; how fast will she go?"

"She timed out at a hair over seventy." Rob stepped closer. "Did you know that an iceboat can travel four times faster than the speed of the wind?"

Rob shook his head while Mr. Enge raised Jim's list to the light. "Runner plank, huh? A good one is mighty necessary when a man is out there maneuvering his way around the course markers."

Mr. Enge paused alongside *Winter Storm*. "Another thing you'll need to watch out for are the chock bolts. They hold the plank to the runner blades. If those are out of alignment, you can forget about winning."

Mr. Enge returned Rob's list. "Can't help you with a ready-made sail, but I have these other things." He led the way to the outside door. "Got a fine laminated Sitka spruce beam that will be perfect for your runner plank. You send Doug around with his pickup and I'll help him load it."

"I'll ask Doug to stop by tonight. About the price—"

"We'll worry about that later. You get the *Snow Devil* repaired and give your friends a good race."

"See you, Mr. Enge."

Rob slid Jim's list into his pocket. Twice Mr. Enge had referred to his classmates as *friends*. How come? Was he blind? They weren't his friends . . . maybe

58

Smitty was . . . sort of a friend. Confused and feeling lonely, Rob closed the door. Was it his fault that he had no friends? Back home . . . back home he had had some really good buddies.

Rob weaved in and around parked cars. If he took the shortcut across the lake, he would save fifteen minutes. Rob knew he would do just about anything to have friends again, guys to ride bikes with, play catch, throw snowballs. He'd do just about anything, he thought, as he swung behind a flatbed truck.

Then he saw Brian Sass with Charlie Ellis.

Rob ducked down.

"Hey," Brian shouted, "who you hiding from?"

Dumb, Rob thought, and straightened slowly. He should walk up to Brian, demand to know what his problem is, just flat out ask, How come you don't like me?

Rob jammed his fists into his coat pockets.

"Is it true," Charlie asked, "that you're going to enter an iceboat in the races?"

"Him, ol' Jelly Ankles?" Brian laughed.

But Charlie persisted. "I saw him leaving the park's office. His name is on the list."

"You're gonna race that piece of rusty junk?" Brian's tone cut through the cold air, and he laughed again.

Rob's face turned hot. Anger welled within him as he stared at the smirk across Brian's face. He wanted to draw back, plant a fist in the middle of Brian's big mouth.

With a low and controlled tone, Rob said, "I'm gonna beat you; beat you and your new DN so bad you won't be able to show your face."

Rob pushed between Brian and Charlie Ellis. He heard them yelling, calling him "Seaweed, Jelly Ankles, Junkman." He heard them laughing too, and calling Doug's boat worthless junk.

When Rob reached home, he rushed through the kitchen, upstairs to his room in spite of his mother's questions. The memory of Brian's laughter continued to sting. Rob threw his coat over the chair. He doubled his fist, jabbed at the mirror.

"Jelly Ankles, Seaweed, Junkman . . ." Rob dove at the pillow. He should take judo, forget about learning to pilot an iceboat; smash Brian Sass like a bug!

As Rob rolled over, he saw the clutter of books on his desk, the colored photo of the *Sun Warrior* . . . a gift, something his dad had bought him. Rob stared at the photograph of the windsurf for a long while, then sat up on the edge of his bed to look at it longer. Decking Brian Sass would be a waste. He had to learn to pilot Doug's boat, become the best in Welholm Falls, then beat Brian so bad he would think he got caught inside a whirlwind.

A knock—the bedroom door opened. Jim filled the rectangle of light. "Rob—"

Rob stared at the man his mom had married. Everyone kept telling him he couldn't do it alone; he knew that he should ask for Jim's help. His help just might make the difference between winning and losing.

Rob wanted to win. He wanted to win more than anything. Shaking now, fighting back the tears, the possibility of losing to Brian and facing a dad who would accept nothing less than winning, Rob blurted, "Some of the guys call me Jelly Ankles and Seaweed. No one likes me . . . especially Brian."

Rob squeezed his eyes shut in hopes of hiding the tears that seeped out beneath his lashes. Was Jim angry because he was crying? Was he ashamed of him? Rob took several quick steps toward Jim's outstretched arms but stopped short.

"I have to win that race," Rob blurted. "I have to!"

Jim moved forward and slid his hands beneath Rob's arms and lifted him up to stand on the bed. He waited until Rob stopped crying. But Rob was slow to face his new dad. He felt awkward, embarrassed, as if he had exposed some secret part of himself. Rob used the sleeve of his shirt to dry his eyes but shied away from the man looking at him.

With his hands still tight around Rob, Jim said, "It was stupid of me not to recognized that something's been bothering you, something other than all of these changes. I thought *I* was the problem, that it would eventually solve itself."

Jim raised Rob's chin. "I've never been a stepdad before. It's sometimes scary when you want the new relationship to be a good one. I've probably done ten things wrong for every right one. I'm sorry, Rob."

This man his mother had married, who kept looking up at him, who kept hanging on to him, apologized as if he had done something wrong. Rob noticed his blue eyes glaze over; he felt the hands that kept holding him steady. Rob tried to pull away. He tried to shrug off Jim's apology.

61

As if sensing Rob's uneasiness, Jim said, "You're a courageous kid, and if it matters, I think you have a lot going for you." Jim paused, allowing time for his words to sink in. "Can we talk, Rob?"

Rob nodded. Jim lifted him down. They sat together on the side of the bed. "You need to know about Brian; you need to understand why he has this illusion about himself. Do you know what an illusion is?"

Rob wasn't sure.

"It's a concept, an opinion, and it seldom has anything to do with what's true." Jim paused, then went on. "Brian's opinion of himself is determined by what he believes others think of him. He drives himself to be the best at everything, thinking that if he is, then his peers will like him. He does this to cover up how bad he feels about himself. He doesn't like himself. For some reason you've become a threat. He couldn't stand it if you did something better. He'd retaliate because, in his mind, you'd be trying to steal his friends." Jim waited. "Do you understand?"

Rob remembered the day last summer, the day at the swimming pool. He remembered how Brian had climbed up to the high board when none of his buddies would; he remembered how they had all booed him when his dive turned into a belly flop; he remembered taking his turn, how silent it got after his perfect half-gainer.

Rob remembered coming up from the bottom of the pool, shaking his head, spitting water, seeing Brian's face. No one could have hated another more. And from that day, it seemed to Rob, Brian had gone out of his way to do those things that made Rob look like a misfit.

"Why?" Rob asked. "Why does he feel that he always has to be best?"

"Do you know about his mother?"

Rob nodded, thinking back to that day in the cafeteria when Jennifer and her friends had been talking about Brian's mom. "I heard that she ran away. What about his dad?"

"He never had one."

. . . *never had a dad, and his mom* . . .

"That's why he lives with his grandmother. She's all the family Brian has, and she gives him things in hopes that those things will somehow make up for his not having a family. Sometimes the things she buys him"—Jim shook his head—"only make Brian's insecurity worse."

"I guess I've always thought that there was something wrong with me."

"There's nothing wrong with you." Jim tousled Rob's hair. "Feel like coming downstairs? Your mother and I have something for you."

Rob used the tail of his shirt to wipe his face. He glanced at his desk, the unopened books, tomorrow's assignments and homework. Rob followed Jim downstairs. The kitchen, bright with overhead lights and yellow-flowered wallpaper, smelled like roast chicken and chocolate cake. His mom smiled but went on setting the dinner table. From the laundry room, Jim produced an armful of packages. "These are for you."

Feelings floated to the surface; Rob pushed them down immediately as his gaze shifted from the packages to the man who gave them.

"Rob," his mother said, "open them."

She placed a hand on his shoulder. For reasons Rob failed to understand, her touch made the gifts acceptable, as if they were from her; she was his mother. And he tore away the wrapping. The box said HELMET. In another he found insulated boots and a set of ice creepers; insulated coveralls in the next.

And his mother said, "I made this myself." The hand-knit face mask was the same cobalt blue as the coveralls. Jagged white streaks that decorated each side of the mask looked like lightning bolts.

"We can't have you getting frostbite," she said, and smiled. Her eyes smiled too.

Rob didn't know why her smile and all the gifts were making him uncomfortable. He couldn't decide if uncomfortable meant guilty, self-pity, or what. So many things were happening to him, forcing him to think about feelings and thoughts he had never had to consider or understand. Was he growing up? Was this what it was like to grow up, to learn to fit in and understand how it all happened?

Rob thanked them for the gifts. He ate his dinner and listened to the others talk, grateful that Doug was always so enthusiastic about everything. Doug liked to talk. He found it easy to see the funny side of everything he did and often made jokes about being a "bumble-head." In some ways Doug reminded him of Smitty. Ms. Pickering said that Smitty was his own person. Rob guessed Doug was his own person too. They both loved their dads; they both wanted to grow up and be like their dads. Is that what being your own person meant? Rob wasn't sure.

Rob excused himself after finishing his chocolate cake and a second glass of milk. He explained that he had homework—vocabulary words and math. As he carried all of the gifts upstairs, he wondered if he wanted to grow up and be just like his dad. He loved his dad. He knew if he could do everything his dad expected of him, he would one day be just as successful.

Rob closed his bedroom door, dumped the gifts into the center of the bed, and stared at them, unsure of why he disliked them. He needed them, he reasoned. Without them he could get frostbite, maybe even freeze stiff. So why all of this . . . Rob didn't know what to call how he felt. He couldn't remember ever feeling like this before. Not ever.

Rob pulled the knitted face mask over his head and studied his reflection in the mirror that was lined with snapshots of his dad. After a moment Rob spun around. He arranged the helmet on the pillow, jerked his mother's gift from his head, and fitted the helmet around it. He spread the insulated overalls the length of the bed, set the insulated boots, toes up, at the bottom of each pant leg. It almost looked like a real person.

Rob backed away from it, from the discomfort churning inside his belly and brain. He backed up until the dresser stopped him. Startled, Rob glanced over his shoulder as if he expected someone to be there. Photos of his dad looked at him—his dad the skier, his dad the golfer, his dad the pilot. Rob grabbed a photo, hurried to the bed, and stuffed it inside of the face mask.

Now it was real . . . his dad the iceboat pilot!

CHAPTER 9

Rob studied the back of Brian's head, one row over and two seats forward. He tried to think of what it would be like not to have a dad, to know that your mother ran away. Probably a guy might wonder if she ran away because she hated him. Probably Jim was right; a guy wouldn't feel very good about himself.

Ms. Pickering's chair scraped against the floor as she pushed it back. She moved to the head of the class. "Charlie Ellis, you have a math assignment due tomorrow. Rob, do you have your vocabulary words?"

Rob blinked. "I forgot."

"Tomorrow morning, right here on my desk."

Rob glanced at the clock—two minutes before 3:00. Ms. Pickering reminded the class of the art project and encouraged them not to leave it until the last minute, then said, "Some of you who never think you can find a suitable book to report on might find Rob's idea helpful." She went on explaining about the book he had chosen, the way in which he had written the report. "Really," she concluded, "it was one of the better papers handed in and Rob impressed me with his knowledge of boats."

Rob felt hot. He looked toward the window as others wrenched around to stare, some smiling, some snickering.

"Brian," Ms. Pickering asked, "will you tell the rest of the class what you find so funny?"

Brian flung his arm back in Rob's direction. "If he knows so much about boats, how come he almost rammed my new DN the other night? He came that close." Brian measured the distance with outstretched arms.

Rob jumped up. "That's not true and you know it!"

"That's enough, Rob. Sit down."

"But it's not true. I didn't come within fifty feet of him."

"Please." Ms. Pickering's long finger pointed at Rob's desk. "Brian, I'm sure you're exaggerating, and something you might remember—there are two kinds of knowledge: one that is learned from doing a thing and the academic kind. They're both necessary for a complete understanding."

Rob's arm shot up.

"Yes," she said, "what is it?"

"In my report, I explained about the parallelogram of forces, which is the phenomenon of a boat being able to sail into the wind." Rob stepped into the aisle and angled his body toward Brian. "I'll bet you can't explain why a boat can sail windward. You just know that it can."

Brian's face turned red.

"That's an excellent example, Rob. I hope all of you understand the difference now in knowing that something will work under certain conditions and understanding why it will work. Rob," she asked, "will you collect the social studies booklets from your section? Jennifer and Charles, in your sections, please."

Rob took his own and the one from the girl just ahead. As he moved forward, gathering those from both sides of the aisle, his foot caught against something that pitched him forward. One desk teetered, another tipped to the floor. Rob rose to his knees, looked up into Brian's threatening eyes.

"I saw it," Jennifer called out. "I saw Brian trip Rob. He stuck his foot out."

"That's a lie; you're a dirty liar."

Ms. Pickering waited until Rob pulled up. "Are you hurt?"

Rob saw the hate on Brian's face, his readiness to fight, the fear that made his cheeks jerk.

"Rob, were you tripped?"

The room went silent. Everyone waited and expected Rob to blame Brian. Remembering what Jim had told him, Rob shrugged. "I could have stumbled. No big deal."

"That's not true, Rob Marshall!" Jennifer stomped her foot. "You know he tripped you."

"Jennifer." Ms. Pickering's voice struck a warning tone.

The bell sounded. "Class dismissed," Ms. Pickering said. "Brian, I'd like you to remain, please."

Rob hurriedly gathered up his books and rushed from the room. Jennifer followed him to the coatrack. "Why did you lie to Ms. Pickering? You know Brian tripped you."

Outside, Rob zipped his coat. "I need to talk to you."

"I saw him do it," Jennifer insisted, and followed Rob across the street. "You're afraid of him."

Jennifer grabbed Rob's sleeve. "You're afraid Brian will punch you out."

"No, Jennifer, I'm not afraid of Brian. I feel sorry for him."

"Feel sorry for Brian?"

Rob explained why as they turned up Lakefront Drive. When he'd finished, he added, "I want to tell you that I'm sorry for scaring you the other night. I scared myself too."

Jennifer raised her chin, obviously trying to decide whether or not to be angry with him.

While he waited for Jennifer's decision, Rob explained why it was so important for him to compete in the festival regatta. "I was being dumb out there and taking chances, but I have to win, Jennifer. My dad expects me to win, to be the best I can be."

Rob shifted his books to the other arm. "I have to hurry and get my homework finished 'cause Jim's going to help me get started tonight with the repairs on Doug's boat."

Rob stopped in front of the Johannsens' house. "I promise to never scare you again or trick you into something you don't want to do."

Jennifer's mouth turned up at the corners. "Can I come over sometime and see what you're doing to Doug's boat?"

"Sure." Rob smiled. "Are we friends?"

Jennifer nodded. "I have my piano lesson," she said. "All of Ms. Swenson's students are playing a combined recital at the festival."

She hurried up the sidewalk while Rob hop-skipped his way into the house. He found a note from his mother that asked him to put the meat loaf into the oven—350 degrees. Rob set the temperature, grabbed a slice of chocolate cake, and rushed upstairs. He wanted to have every bit of homework done by the time Jim got home. If he fell behind in his schoolwork, he knew his mother would end his iceboat dreams faster than he could say "Please don't."

CHAPTER 10

Immediately after dinner Rob followed Jim to the boathouse and helped Doug unload the spruce beam. Then, with pencils and tablets of unlined paper, they sat down to sketch the *Snow Devil*'s basic design. Besides measuring the length of the fuselage, the runner plank, the distance it set back from the steering runner, Rob listened to Jim and Doug discuss the merits of moving the runner plank. "I think moving it back a couple of inches will give the boat more stability."

"Good idea," Doug said. "Those strong gusts that come across the lake play havoc with a guy's steering."

"The wind," Jim said to Rob, "is sometimes the pilot's toughest opponent."

"Tougher than Brian and his new DN?" Rob asked.

"Don't be frightened by that new DN. It might possibly be too much boat for Brian. It won't allow him many mistakes. Now," Jim said, "let's get this boat rebuilt."

Doug measured out plywood for the new fuselage. Jim cut it, then gave Rob an electric sander and showed him how to use it. It vibrated inside his hand as he moved it up and down the plywood. Rob liked the smell of the freshly cut wood. It reminded him of mountains and the fun time he'd had with Jennifer and her family, the canoeing trip he and Doug had taken while his mom and Jim were on their honeymoon.

"How's it coming?" Jim asked, as he set a kettle of cider onto the potbellied stove in the back of the boathouse. "Good job." And he ran his fingertips the length of the plywood strip.

As Rob finished sanding each piece, Doug took it, placed it on sawhorses, and drilled new screw holes. Jim passed out cups of cider, occasionally supervised, but spent most of the evening cutting and shaping the spruce beam so that it formed a convex upward arc.

Scents of pine and spruce, cider and glue filled the boathouse along with the whir of machinery and the wind slashing across the lake. Doug reminisced about projects he and his dad had shared, laughed, and kept asking, "Do you remember?"

Rob enjoyed listening to the stories, enjoyed the kidding that went back and forth between them, and it made Rob think about his own dad. Either he was away on business or he was too busy. There never seemed to be time for doing things together, like projects, roughing it in the mountains, or the good-natured kind of exchange that Rob saw between Doug and his dad. Rob envied Doug. He knew why Doug loved his dad, knew why he wanted to grow up to be just like him.

Jim rested a hand on Rob's shoulder as they took time to drink the cider and watch Doug glue the plywood, clamp it together, then drive the screws into place. Rob smiled as the new fuselage took shape. "Looks great," he said, wondering if Doug would paint it the same black color as the old one.

"Is it okay if I sand on the beam?" Rob asked.

"Good idea," Jim answered, and gave Rob a wink.

Outside the wind continued to blow. Sometimes a gust hit the boathouse, rattled down the stovepipe, and forced a thin trail of gray, maple-scented smoke into the warm room. Rob liked the smell of it; he liked working with tools and the feeling of being trusted with a piece of really expensive equipment. Rob had never helped build anything before, never worked with more than a screwdriver and pliers. When Jim complimented him, Rob felt the pleasure of it swell inside his chest, and he began to whistle.

Doug whistled too. Sometimes he sang, really loud, then he laughed. Jim would smile, shake his head, then go back to smoothing the spruce beam. The sounds, the smells, the sensations all meshed into one, into a neat kind of happiness that Rob had never experienced. It made him feel good, and he was sorry when Doug finished putting the fuselage together. And Jim said, "I think it's time to call it a night."

Doug used solvent to clean his hands. "This is gonna be a brand-new boat. And a new boat," he said, "deserves a new name. What's it gonna be, Rob?"

Rob looked up at his new dad, saw him nod. "That's right, Rob. This is your boat."

The fact that Doug was giving away his boat left Rob speechless. The fact that Jim was letting him have it muddled Rob's brain, and the only name he could think of was *Snow Devil*—the name painted on the side of the old fuselage. "Can I think about it?"

"Twenty-four hours," Doug barked, laughing at the same time.

Jim rested a hand on Rob's shoulder. "I promised your mother I wouldn't let this project interfere with your schoolwork."

"I could work all night. I'm not one bit tired."

"If you did," Jim said, "I'd be in big trouble with your mom."

"We'll have it ready for you to take out this weekend," Doug said.

"No kidding!"

"That's right," Jim added. "You've been a big help. You handle tools really well."

"I've had a good time. It's been fun."

Doug gave Rob a good-natured elbow. "Just wait until Dad makes you clean up the place."

"I'll do it. I'll do it right now."

"No, you won't." Jim laughed, switching off the light.

The wind left snowdrifts across the backyard. It followed them to the house and came inside until Jim closed it out.

Rob thought about the boat and what he might name it, until he dropped off to sleep. He dreamed about winning a trophy bigger than he was. The next day in school all of Rob's doodles were in the shapes of sails stretched taut by wind and driving snow that continued to slash across the lake.

On the hurried walk home, Rob told Jennifer about the boat he had had when he lived in California. "I called it the *Sun Warrior.*"

Jennifer wrinkled her nose.

"That's a good name," Rob cried.

"It sounds silly."

"What's so silly about it?"

Jennifer stopped in front of her house. "If I had a sailboat, I'd name it the *Breezy Dancer*, and if I had an iceboat, which I don't want, I'd name it something cold."

"Like what?"

"Something like frigid or frosty. Maybe I'd call it *Arctic Night.*"

"Well," Rob said, drawing his shoulders up around his ears, "Doug gave me the boat and told me to think of a name. I've decided to call it the *Ice Warrior.*"

Then Rob hurried off; he wanted to have the boathouse swept clean before Jim got home.

CHAPTER 11

"Ice Warrior," Jim said, and closed the door on the potbellied stove, the fire rumbling inside. "It's a good name; fits the pilot."

Rob shifted his attention from the wire brush and chock bolts to the man warming his hands in the steam that rose from inside the kettle of cider. What exactly had Jim meant—"fits the pilot"? A wisecrack?

"You have a lot of courage," Jim said. "Rebuilding this boat, wanting to compete with very little experience is a big undertaking. Not for the faint of heart."

Rob liked the compliment. He should say something, like thanks, maybe. But every thought got tripped up with the blood rushing to his face. He bent lower over the chock bolts.

"We'll need to get the runners sharpened and the fuselage painted," Jim said. "You'll want to be out on that lake this weekend, practicing."

". . . on the lake this weekend"? Rob wanted to laugh as he envisioned head-high drifts, subarctic temperatures, and sixty-knot winds. Not only was the weather against him but Ms. Pickering kept reminding everyone of the art project. "Something that depicts the spirit of Winter Festival" was the last thing she had said. Could he hand in the *Ice Warrior* just long enough for a grade? Jim said he had courage. Would Ms. Pickering think the *Ice Warrior* and his courage were in the spirit of Winter Festival?

Sure she would!

Without Doug around, the boathouse was quiet, sometimes awkward. Rob felt he should be talking, joking around the way Doug joked around. His dad said he'd been born without a sense of humor. "Too serious," his dad often said. "You're just like your mother, can't take a joke."

His dad's voice got mixed up with the wind blowing outside and the whir of Jim's sander until the voice and the man drifted away. Rob followed his thoughts onto the ice. He imagined the *Ice Warrior* as sleek and swift as Brian's new DN. He thought about the racecourse, iceboats lined up and waiting. He thought about his dad watching.

Would his mom invite his dad to sit in the stands with her and Jim? Would his dad do it? Would they talk to one another? What kinds of things would she say?

And his dad? Of course he'd shake hands with Jim, call him by his first name, act as if they'd been best friends forever. "Business is fantastic. Bought a new airplane, flying to Mazatlán. Met this Mexican when I was down there fishing with the CEO; hit it off right away. He owns a fleet of fishing boats. Great guy. I gave him some tips on how to computerize his whole operation. We're talking about my buying into his business. Terrific opportunity."

Rob let the air from his lungs in a long, gradual sigh. His dad, the businessman—always on top of every opportunity, always the success.

"Rob"—Jim's voice broke into his thoughts—"what do you think? Think this runner plank is ready to paint?"

Rob set the wire brush aside, moved to the other side of the room, and ran his fingertips along the spruce beam. "Feels okay to me."

"What color would you like it painted?"

"Orange," he answered. "Every time I think about it, it's orange. The *Sea Warrior* was orange like the sun just before it drops off the far edge of the Pacific. Sometimes I'd hang around Point Loma just to watch the sun go down." Rob caught himself talking too much. "The chock bolts are done. What's next?"

"You miss California, don't you?"

Rob nodded. "How 'bout if I clean up?"

"Sounds good to me. Soon as I finish drilling the runner plank we'll call it a night."

Rob took the push broom down from the hook. He started in the corner, alongside the tight-fitting double door. He felt the heat of the stove, heard the hiss from the kettle of cider, smelled the sweet aroma of apples, cinnamon, and cloves. Wind rattled the stovepipe. The whir of Jim's drill and the crackling of wood burning inside the stove surrounded Rob with a good kind of feeling. And allowed Rob's thoughts to take a new direction.

He had never thought much about the kind of man he wanted to be one day. He supposed that he just thought he'd grow up and be the kind of man his dad expected him to be. His dad told him to get into business: "That's where the money is. When the time comes, and you're ready, I'll pull a few strings."

Rob's grip tightened on the broom handle. Did a son have to believe what his dad believed? Did he have to grow up and be that same kind of man? Jim wasn't like his own dad. Rob doubted that Jim had ever pulled any strings, done anything just for the money.

"Big bucks is what makes the world turn, and don't you forget it." Rob remembered his dad saying that. It was one of his favorite lines.

Rob had never thought of himself as being able to build anything. If you wanted something, you went to a store and bought it. He had always thought of men who worked with their hands as being somehow less than men who used their brains. "The guys with the brains are the guys with the big bucks."

Big bucks and no time for anything but business, Rob thought.

Rob liked using his hands—feeling the vibrations of the machinery inside his fingers, then crawling up his arms. He liked seeing a piece of wood become something usable. Liked the satisfaction of stepping back, looking at his work, and knowing he had done it. Would his dad understand that?

Jim would. Jim referred to Mr. Enge and Smitty's dad as real craftsmen, with the same tone of voice as Rob's dad used to praise the CEO who pulled off a big deal. Rob had met some of his own dad's friends, men involved in their professions, always talking about deals and tax shelters, interest rates and bottom lines. Jim talked about other things: like the kind of courage it took to compete in the Iditarod, ways the city could finance a speedway course for guys like Doug to race their cars, reasons for Brian Sass's behavior, and about building iceboats.

Rob pushed the broom into the corner, cleaned up the trash, and dumped it into the basket. His dad and Jim operated in different worlds. Being around Jim had shown Rob this other world.

"Think we'll be able to get the fuselage and runner plank over to Smitty's dad? This storm . . ."

Jim tousled Rob's hair. "Doug and I'll drop it off in the morning on our way to school. Don't worry; you'll be out there practicing this weekend."

The wind and blowing snow outside, the parts and pieces of the *Ice Warrior* spread out over the boathouse floor, strained Rob's imagination. Would he be practicing Saturday morning? Could he learn enough to win the DN Amateur Class Race? Would his winning please his dad?

Rob thought of little else when he went to school the next day. At recess Smitty told him that Doug and Jim had dropped off the fuselage and runner plank on their way to school. At noon Rob told Jennifer that Jim was going to set the runner plank back a few inches to give the boat more stability, but Jennifer didn't care. And Rob wasn't interested in hearing about the diorama she was making for her art project. On the way home she asked Rob about his project.

"I'm going to hand in the *Ice Warrior*."

"You can't do that. A boat doesn't have anything to do with art." Jennifer turned her head away from the blowing snow. "Want to stop off at my house and see my diorama?"

"Can't. Mom's taking me to Mr. Enge's place to pick up the material for my sail."

"Can I come?"

"Sure," Rob said, and saw his mother backing out the car from the garage.

They ran. Rob slid in the front seat. Jennifer squeezed in beside him. "This weather," his mother said, as she tuned in the weather station.

Each time the weatherman spoke of continued snow, his mother groaned a little sound that Rob took to mean she wished she was back in San Diego. Rob did too. But then, he didn't. He wanted to pilot the *Ice Warrior*. He wanted to whip Brian Sass, wanted to get that trophy, and show his dad that he was a winner too. But it had to stop snowing.

Rob looked out at the slick, snow-packed street, at the snow whipping slant-wise in front of the car. It gave every indication of going on forever.

Late last summer when Rob moved to town, the main street of Welholm Falls had been lined with big green trees, like umbrellas across the street. Now those same trees looked dead, like spooks with crooked arms, while the strands of Christmas lights looked like spiderwebs. "How come they haven't taken down the lights?" he asked.

"They will just as soon as the festival is over," Jennifer replied. "They'll turn them back on for Festival Weekend."

"If it doesn't stop snowing," Rob said, "people won't be able to get out of their houses."

"I heard the storm is going to last until Monday."

"Monday!" Rob groaned. "You have to be wrong, Jennifer. This town will be buried by Monday."

Rob's mom drew up in front of Mr. Enge's store. "Button up those coats and hurry."

Rob slid out behind Jennifer, ran ahead, and threw open the door. A rush of warm air and music from a radio drifted toward him. "Mr. Enge," Rob called.

"Nobody's here," Jennifer said. "This place is spooky. Let's leave."

The old barn was empty of people, full of shadows, strange smells, and creaking sounds. Rob called again.

"Back here."

"That's Mr. Enge. Come on, Jennifer, you got to see his iceboat. It's a beauty."

Rob hurried ahead. Jennifer acted less than enthusiastic, and for a moment Rob lost patience and wondered why she had asked to come along. "What brings you two out on a day like this?" Mr. Enge asked.

"I need to pick up the Dacron for my sail." Rob pulled the square of paper from his pocket, read off the dimensions.

"Sorry," he said. "I don't have a yard of Dacron left."

"My mom said nylon would do."

"No nylon either. I've been sending folks to Johnson's Fabric Center, but I understand he's sold out too."

"What'll I do? I need a sail."

"You might try the boat supply in Logan's Harbor but call first. No sense having your folks drive that thirty miles in weather like this unless you know they have what you want."

Rob turned to Jennifer. "Good thing Mom's with us. We can leave for Logan's Harbor right now. Thanks, Mr. Enge."

"If they don't have it," he called out, "the only other place you might be able to find it is in Demmering."

Jennifer followed Rob outside. They raced to the car. "Mr. Enge is all out of fabric, Mom. We have to go to Logan's Harbor right now."

"Logan's Harbor? That's a thirty-mile trip."

"Logan's Harbor is only fifteen miles."

"Fifteen miles each way," his mother answered.

"We have to go now, Mom. If we wait around for this storm to pass, they might sell out too."

"Do you have any idea what the highway must be like?"

"You're a good driver. You can take it easy."

"No."

"Mom!"

"I'm sorry, Rob. I'm not taking the car any farther than home."

"If I don't have a sail for my boat, I can't race it."

"Maybe you should call the store in Logan's Harbor like Mr. Enge said."

"Good idea, Jennifer." Rob's mom turned the car toward home.

Rob frowned. He wanted to drive to Logan's Harbor right now, not telephone. And he grew impatient with his mother's driving. It was taking forever. If his dad was behind the wheel, he'd blast his way through the drifts. Be home in ten seconds.

"Do you know how much cloth you need?" his mother asked as she turned onto Lakefront.

Rob read off the dimensions. He kept the slip of paper in his hand. He saw the garage door go up, heard his mother say, "I'll ask them to hold the material until Jim can drive me over on Saturday."

"Saturday will be too late," Rob protested. "I have to be on the lake practicing Saturday morning."

"Why can't you use the old sail?" Jennifer asked.

Rob glared at her, wanted to tell Jennifer to mind her own business. But once the car stopped inside the garage, he was out and running to the house. He grabbed the phone off the hook, pushed it at his mother.

She called information, then dialed. "Yes," she said, "do you carry Dacron or nylon by the yard? It's for a boat sail."

A long moment passed. "Oh," she said. "Then perhaps you can suggest another place. I'm calling from Welholm Falls."

Again she paused. "Demmering? Isn't there a place closer than Demmering?"

Rob felt a sudden pain in the middle of his belly as he watched his mother replace the receiver. "They're out of the cloth, Rob. She said the mill that supplies the fabric has been on strike for the past three months. She has no idea when they'll receive another shipment or who might have any in stock."

Rob turned away. What good was it going to do to have the best and fastest iceboat on the lake if he couldn't get a sail to make it go? And what would his dad say? "Excuses are for losers."

CHAPTER 12

Snow stopped falling Friday during recess. By afternoon, patches of blue pushed their way through the gray. The weather forecast called for sunny skies but cold.

Rob was the first one out of his classroom, first one out of the building. He ran home and finished his homework before dinner. Jim didn't make any promises, but he said that he had a friend living in Demmering. "I'll give Don a call. If anyone can find sailcloth, he can."

"And," his mother said, "just as soon as I have the cloth, I'll make the sail."

"Terrific," Doug added. "I have a date and I could use a hand unloading the *Ice Warrior.*"

"You got it already?" Rob asked. "How does it look?"

"Like an orange Popsicle."

Rob reached the back of Doug's pickup first. "Wow!" he exclaimed. "It's beautiful."

Once the runner plank and fuselage were inside the

boathouse and the door closed, Rob moved close to the stove, to stand opposite his new dad. "I want to thank you," he said, his gaze fixed on the soot-blackened kettle. "I appreciate all that you've done"—Rob extended his hands over the heat like Jim did—"and I've had a great time doing it."

There were other things Rob thought about saying. But what his own dad did and didn't do would be of no interest to Jim. And Rob doubted that he could explain about the hurt he felt inside his chest whenever he let himself compare his two dads.

"You've done a good job," Jim said. "You handle tools well and you have a sense about what needs to be done. Not everyone has that." A gentle smile spread over Jim's face. "What do you think of the color? I told Barney—that's Smitty's dad—that you wanted it the color of a setting California sun."

"It's perfect. Just like Doug said—an orange Popsicle."

Jim laughed. "What do you say we put the *Ice Warrior* back together? You'll want to get an early start in the morning."

They worked until just past midnight. It was as beautiful a boat as Brian's factory-built DN. And the next morning, alone at the breakfast table with his mom, he tried to tell her how working in the boathouse made him feel.

He liked handling tools; they felt comfortable inside his hand. "Like maybe I was born knowing what to do with them." He liked the sawing and sanding, taking the wood down one thin layer at a time until it took on a shape of its own, until the grain began to show through and gave the piece its own face. "The longer I work out there, the more comfortable I feel. I want to take some shop courses next year. I want to get really good at making things."

"That's the first time I've heard you talk about what you want to do. You've always just gone along with whatever was happening at the moment."

Rob moved the muffin papers from one side of his plate to the other. "Seems like I just started thinking about things, like how I feel. I don't understand a lot that's happening inside me, why I feel like I feel, why I'm thinking about things I've never thought about before. I'm not even sure of the words to put with the feelings."

She reached across, pressed her hand over his. "I think it's called growing up."

"I don't feel grown up. Whenever Doug is around I feel like a little kid."

"You're twelve going on thirteen. Doug is seventeen."

"Yeah, driving his own car, dating girls, planning on going away to college next year, living alone."

"You'll be doing those same things one day."

Rob nodded. "Mom, do you miss California?"

"Sometimes."

"Me too. Everything was really easy for me out there. Had neat friends. I was good at swimming and diving. I could do things with my windsurf that—" Rob rolled his lips together. "Well, I was really good, Mom."

"And you're going to do just fine here. Look at what

you've accomplished already—new friends, the iceboat, hockey."

"I'm a bust at hockey. Even the ten-year-olds are better than me. And I don't have friends like I had at home."

"What about Jennifer?"

"She's a girl."

"Oh, is that right?"

"Mom, come on. You know what I mean."

"No, I don't. Why can't a girl be a good friend?"

"They're different."

"Why, because they don't agree with everything you say and think? Their thoughts and feelings are just as important as boys'." She drew back her hand. "When two boys are together and think exactly alike, what's to be learned? It's like looking at a car from just one side. Think what else you might learn about the car if you moved around and looked at it from the front—a whole different perspective, right?"

Rob raised an eyebrow, thinking the conversation sounded like some of the arguments his mom and dad used to have over the Sunday newspaper. Rob pushed back from the table. "Think I better get going. I got a lot of practicing to do."

"Jim said that he will catch up with you just as soon as he gets back from the dentist. He also said that you are to check the ice for cracks and thickness before you take the boat out. Please be careful."

"It's a great day. Sunshine, no wind, a new boat. It can't get any better."

Before Rob left the house, he slipped into all the

new clothes his mother and Jim had given him. He even smiled as he hurried down to the boathouse, thinking that he now walked with a kind of swagger, walked the way Doug walked.

Rob opened the boathouse door. His boat looked back at him like a warrior, he thought. He wanted to push it out, get started, but Jim's warning about shell ice and places on the snow-covered surface that looked different rang in his ears.

Rob made a quarter-mile figure eight out from the boathouse before he saw two other boats bearing down on him. Smitty's *Windy Demon* reached him first. Smitty waved. "Your boat looks really terrific. My dad couldn't believe it was Doug's old boat. What are you doing out here? What's wrong with your boat?"

Before Rob could answer, the *Annihilator* came swooshing in, then Brian brought his boat about, using the hand brake to effect the abrupt stop.

"I'm checking for shell ice. Jim say that ice can freeze on top but leave a cavity of air or water beneath it."

Brian hooted. "It's fifteen below. It's been below twenty for the last week."

Rob's fingers pulled back and made fists inside his black gloves. Rob tried to remember everything Jim had told him about Brian, why he acted the way he did, that he was really someone to feel sorry for, that he called other people names and tried to belittle them to make himself feel superior. But Rob didn't care about Brian's problems, why he did what he did. He wanted to bust his nose.

Rob took a step back. Maybe Jennifer was right, maybe he was afraid of Brian. He stood a few inches taller than any of the other guys, weighed less than Smitty, but in the insulated coveralls and behind the weird face mask, Brian looked like a monster.

Brian removed his helmet, then his face mask. His hair was too long, greasy, not clean enough. His teeth were crooked, the front two chipped. His eyes were like marbles, cold and hard. Brian pulled out of the cockpit, shook his legs, took a few taunting steps toward Rob. Gray vapor, like smoke from a smoldering fire, rose between them.

"I hear that you're tellin' everyone you're a better pilot than I am, that you're gonna beat me."

A chill raced the length of Rob's spine. He tried to understand the sudden hollow feeling in the pit of his stomach. Jennifer *was* right! Brian did scare him. The idea of slugging it out scared him.

Rob swallowed deep. "That's right," he answered. "I'm just as good a pilot as you."

"You're nothing but dog scraps." Brian stepped closer. "Go get your boat, Junkman. Let's see if you can beat me."

"I'll race you at Winter Festival."

"Too chicken to race me now?" Brian threw back his head, calling to Smitty, "He's all talk."

Rob knew he should back away, get on with checking the safety of the ice, but he noticed Smitty watching. Was he thinking Rob was chicken too?

"Come on, Marshall. I'll even give you a head start."

"I'll race you Festival Weekend."

91

"Chicken," Brian chanted. "If you think you're so good, race me now. Prove it. Prove that you're not all talk."

A smirk spread across Brian's face. "What's the matter—haven't you read far enough in your library book? Bet you don't even know how to work the sheet."

"I can work it just fine."

"Talk, that's what you do best. Even Smitty says you're a big talker."

Rob glanced sideways, caught and held the redhead's eyes. Should he believe Brian? Did Smitty think he was just a bunch of words? Rob's fists doubled tighter. "Okay, I'll race you."

Brian pulled the face mask back over his head. "I'll meet you on the ice across from the park in forty-five minutes unless you chicken out."

"Wait up, Rob," Smitty called.

"You go with Junkman," Brian threatened, "and you're no friend of mine."

Smitty waved Brian off, yelled for Rob to stop. "You really going to race Brian?"

"Do you think I'm just a lot of talk like Brian said?"

"Brian's got a big mouth and he makes up the truth to suit himself," Smitty answered. "I'm not sure if a guy can read a few books, then go out on the ice and be a whiz-bang pilot, but you got guts. And I think you're too smart to let Brian sucker you into this stupid race."

"So what should I do? You know what he'll tell everyone at school."

"He's been making cracks about you since that day

last summer at the swimming pool. That was the best half-gainer I've ever seen anyone make, even better than Doug's."

"Thanks, but I've really had it with Brian calling me stupid names."

"So bust him in the mouth. He might even get to like you."

Rob failed to understand Smitty's reasoning, but he accepted his offer of a ride home. "Let's get your boat and go out to the east end of the lake. That's far enough away that Brian won't come looking for us, and maybe I can give you a few tips."

"Sounds like a great idea, but I have to leave word with my mom. Jim's coming out on the snowmobile later." Rob laughed. "Maybe between the two of you, I can learn enough to beat Brian."

CHAPTER 13

"Meet you at the east end," Smitty yelled after giving the *Ice Warrior* a starting push.

Rob waved his thanks, then settled into the two-seat cockpit. He adjusted the sheet until the sail swung taut and in proper trim. He pressed both knees against the tiller. Nothing stood before him now except the empty sweeps of snow and sky. Rob set his course on that distant line where sky and snow touched—a long, vaporous gray ribbon.

He glanced over his shoulder as the *Ice Warrior* picked up speed. A boat-length separated his boat from Smitty's. Rob smiled.

Wind, cold that caught in his throat, puffs of vapor that escaped his mouth and fogged his visor, grew into a tremor that pushed out against his chest. He was alone, in command of a craft that could easily hurtle him northward faster than his courage could keep up. The tremor exploded into fragments of tingly excitement that shot into every part of his body. He smiled again.

Little by little, Rob increased his lead. He thought about hiking the boat, turning the sail closer to the wind. He had to test himself, test his ability and courage—push himself beyond that line of fear his dad always talked about: "A man must continually test himself, find the limit of his courage, then push himself beyond that." Rob adjusted the sail another quarter of an inch. The *Ice Warrior* surged ahead. There was a race to win, a trophy to hold up for his dad to see and everyone in Welholm Falls too. See! Look what the California kid can do!

The iron-on patches glistened against the brilliant morning light. Wind rippled the sail. Runners left behind their song as they cut across the ice and through the snow. Sensations stirred within him. He felt like a magician, nothing was impossible, and he adjusted the sheet again.

The *Ice Warrior* shuddered as it shot still farther ahead. Was his boat a better boat? Was he as good a pilot as he believed he was? Did he possess those special instincts that his dad said every champion must have?

A shiver ran the length of Rob's spine—a wonderfully cold and exhilarating shiver that teased him to go faster. He had the wind, sweeps of empty space, a solid sheet of ice. Nothing could stop him. Faster! Discover those instincts that every champion must possess.

Rob felt the *Ice Warrior* flying, barely skimming the surface on razor-sharp runners. His speed, the wind, it felt as if he were being catapulted into space, and he screamed as all the pent-up energy pressing against his chest finally came crashing out of his mouth. Faster!

Faster.

Splinters of ice, slivers of cold found their way through the hand-knit face mask and stung his cheeks. He had to be traveling sixty at least!

Sixty?

Rob remembered what Smitty had said about the winds. They could come out of nowhere. They were unforgiving. Rob awakened to that line within him. That place where courage stopped and fear took over.

His fingers locked around the sheet. Half of his brain pushed to go faster, test himself, experience the excitement of flying through white, frozen space. The other half of his brain overflowed with doubt.

He was a beginner!

The wind suddenly became his enemy, pushing him beyond his limits. Rob trembled. His knees quivered. His brain short-circuited. But his instincts took charge, and he brought the sheet back an eighth of an inch, then another.

The sail crackled. It snapped as the *Ice Warrior* came about. Stopped. Rob reached down to set the hand brake. His fingers refused to bend. Every muscle in his body felt as if it might tear, leaving his heart and lungs to come crashing through his chest.

Rob jumped free of the cockpit. Set the parking brake. He turned in a circle. His brain spun like a gyroscope gone crazy, and he ran back to meet Smitty.

"Man," Smitty shouted, "you were flying."

Rob nodded. "It was wild."

96

"You're just lucky you didn't catch a gust. Fast as you were going you'd have done a three-sixty flip, bust the *Ice Warrior* into a million pieces." Smitty shook his head. "You got guts, I'll say that for you."

"But not much sense" was what Rob knew Smitty wanted to say. And Smitty would have been right. Testing himself, finding the limit of his courage was one thing, but jeopardizing the *Ice Warrior* had been stupid. "Going that fast," Rob admitted, "wasn't very smart. You still want to give me a few pointers?"

"Sure, and the first thing I want to tell you is that Brian is always doing what you just did. He likes to show off when he's racing. He takes lots of dumb chances."

"Is that what you think I was doing—showing off and taking dumb chances?"

"Can't say," Smitty answered. "I don't know you all that well. For right now, I'd like to think that you got carried away with the speed and excitement. My dad says speed is real addictive."

"I never felt anything like it before."

Rob wanted to explain more, but Smitty said, "You started out really great. You have to get the jump on Brian right off or you'll be in big trouble."

"How come?"

"He likes to intimidate guys he doesn't know. With his new boat he'll try intimidating everyone in the race, so you have to get out ahead of him. Brian isn't a good sport when it comes to winning or losing. He doesn't exactly break the rules, but he sure bends them and always to his advantage. It's each guy for himself."

Smitty pushed his helmet to the back of his head.

97

"Brian likes to start off on a windward course and get a big lead. His tacking is sloppy. To make up for that, he crowds his opponents as they come up from behind, hoping they'll make a mistake and beat themselves."

"If the winds are like you say, I can see how easy it would be to foul up."

"Let's head back," Smitty said. "I'll stay up close and off to starboard. If you see me waving, pull up, okay?"

"Sure thing." Rob hurried back to the *Ice Warrior*. He released the parking brake, then reached inside the cockpit and freed the hand brake.

He pushed the *Ice Warrior* ahead, vaulted into the cockpit with a sudden surge of confidence. He had tested himself, done a really stupid thing and survived. He promised himself that he'd never let the excitement of speed take control of his good sense. There was more to winning than being fast.

CHAPTER 14

Rob was surprised when he saw Jim coming across the lake in the snowmobile, surprised that it was noon already. Nor could he believe that Jennifer was riding behind and holding the basket his mom used for taking a picnic lunch to the beach.

But why not? And he brought the *Ice Warrior* around. Hopped out, set the parking brake, set the *Windy Demon*'s brake when Smitty pulled nearby. "This is great," Rob shouted. "An arctic picnic."

"You California guys don't have everything." Smitty laughed, gave Rob a good-natured jab as they jogged toward the snowmobile.

Jim pushed his goggles onto his forehead. "Thought you fellas might be getting hungry."

"I've been running on empty for the last hour," Smitty said. "Rob wouldn't stop."

Smitty took the picnic basket; Rob gave Jennifer a

hand as she slid off the snowmobile. Everything about Jennifer was pink—insulated coveralls, mittens, face mask, stocking cap—everything. "I thought you didn't like iceboating."

He couldn't be sure if Jennifer stuck her nose in the air and ignored his question or hadn't heard. Every part of her was insulated against the subzero temperature with at least three layers of pink.

"There's soup in the thermos, and hot cider," Jim said, passing out cups, then sandwiches.

"This is a feast," Smitty said. "Ms. Erikson's a good cook."

"And," Jim said, "Jennifer made brownies after she came home from her piano lesson. She's a good cook too."

Rob took a brownie, stuffed it into his mouth while Jim filled his cup with soup. The brownie was good—chewy, and it stuck to Rob's teeth just the way he liked. He reached for another.

Arctic picnics were different from those on the beach at Coronado. Instead of sandy bologna sandwiches and snow cones, Rob ate stiff tuna-fish sandwiches, drank hot cider. He kept stomping his feet, rolling his lips together to keep his front teeth warm. Sounded crazy—keeping his teeth warm, but Rob laughed a lot. He ate almost as much as Smitty ate. Jim said they both ate as much as baby elephants. But Jennifer disagreed. "I think they ate as much as full-grown elephants."

"It's 'cause you and Rob's mom are such terrific cooks."

Smitty grinned and split the last brownie with Rob while Jim talked about various tricks of handling a sheet. Afterward, he motioned both boys back into their boats. "Jennifer and I will follow alongside in the snowmobile. I want you fellas to do a couple of tacks, then stop. We'll talk about your technique."

Each time they stopped, Jim offered pointers on ways to maintain their speed and smooth out their tacks. He used terms like *best angle, push, play*. He said there were two sets of rules that a fellow should follow: one for competition racing, the other for having fun.

Rob felt as if his mind would spill over while Smitty nodded and took in every word. Rob knew Smitty understood. To beat Smitty, he knew he would have to get lucky.

Jim said that luck sometimes played a big part in iceboat racing—crosswinds, starting position, abilities, and the lack of abilities.

"Lots of unexpected things can happen," Jim added. "Wind shifts and gusts can be a racer's toughest opponents. But try not to panic. When you see the boat ahead of you hike, get ready, because that same wind gust is going to hit you. Start your turn and you'll be able to ride it out."

He talked about collisions and made a point of telling about pilots who crowded other boats.

"Brian does that all the time," Smitty said.

"He does it to win," Jennifer added. "Brian thinks he has to win at everything."

"One of these times," Jim said, "when he's running

too close to another boat, a gust will come along, hike his craft, and cause him to swerve into another boat."

He warned about crossing paths on opposite tacks too. "You may be on a starboard tack and have the right of way to cut across another boat's bow. But if that other pilot doesn't know the rule, that he's to give way, or chooses not to follow the rules, then there's going to be a collision. Tonight," Jim told Rob, as he started back to the snowmobile, "we'll sit down after dinner and go over the rules."

Jennifer waved good-bye while Rob and Smitty gave their boats a starting push. Though the temperature continued to drop and the sky turned gray, Rob and Smitty spent the remainder of the afternoon practicing, perfecting those maneuvers that Jim had taught them.

Later, just before Smitty pushed off for home, he said, "You've got a good shot at beating Brian; you've caught on really fast."

"Am I good enough to beat you?" Rob asked.

"If you end up beating me"—Smitty grinned—"then Jim and I are fantastic teachers. See you, Rob."

He liked Smitty, liked him as well as any of the guys he'd left behind in California. Maybe he even liked Smitty best of all. Rob closed the boathouse doors and ran for the house.

After dinner, and while his mother cleared away the dishes, Jim sketched out the racecourse on a sheet of paper and took Rob through the mechanics of upwind and downwind strategy. "You'll need to keep track of your opponents too. Know where they are. Never follow behind another boat or to leeward. You'll be in his turbulence and lose speed. Either pinch up to windward or bear off to leeward. You'll pick up speed, so get around him and give yourself the choice of where you want to start your first tack."

Rob's mind spun in circles. Would he remember all that Jim and Smitty had told him, remember it long enough to practice, then do it automatically?

"Do you two know what time it is?" His mother pointed to the kitchen clock. "And there is church in the morning."

They both pushed back from the table. Rob followed Jim to the stairway. "One last thing, Rob. It's something I tell my students: Before you ever begin something new, spend a lot of time thinking about it, picture yourself doing it. Before you go to sleep tonight, see yourself out there in your boat going through each of the maneuvers you learned today. Remember the feel of the sheet inside your hand, exactly how you worked the tiller with your knees. Think about the wind, how it felt when it hit the *Ice Warrior*, how you reacted, what you did to compensate to keep your boat steady. Think about hitting a rock on the ice and how you'll respond, or about another boat coming up on your windward side." Jim paused. "What you have to do is coordinate your mind with each action. It has to be as close to simultaneous as you can make it. Understand?"

"Yes, sir."

Jim gave Rob's shoulder a squeeze. "You learn fast; you're a good student."

But could he cram a whole winter's worth of experience into the few remaining days? Could he win the Amateur Class Race, bring home the trophy? And his dad . . . would he realize the improbability of a guy beating others who had four and five years of racing experience, or would he just expect his son to win?

Rob knew how hard his dad worked to be a winner, how important winning was to him, proving that he was the *best*.

"Winning isn't everything, Rob. It's the only thing."

Rob remembered when his dad had taken up skiing. He'd bought books, taken lessons, rented videos. Every weekend had been spent on the slopes, every conversation had been about skiing. He'd thrown the words around like he had spent his life on skis.

Once his dad got hooked on a thing, there was never time for anything else. He'd been that same way about flying, golf too. Maybe that's how it had to be for a guy to be a winner.

CHAPTER 15

Sunday morning Rob asked to stay home from church. "Homework," he told his mother, then realized his mistake.

Immediately after returning from the morning service, she shooed him upstairs. Rob wandered about his room—desk to dresser to window. Mr. Johannsen shoveled snow from the sidewalk next door. Bend over, push the shovel ahead, raise up, throw the snow aside. Then he began again: Bend over, push the shovel ahead, raise it up, throw the snow aside. Slow, each move deliberate, precise. Rob couldn't picture his dad shoveling snow, couldn't picture him ever living in a place like Welholm Falls. His dad liked excitement, liked variety, things to do. Sure, people went fishing in Welholm Falls, iceboating in the winter. Smitty's dad raced cars in the summer, and everyone in town watched all the high school games, the VFW summer baseball series. Rob removed his dad's note from the desk drawer. There were no fancy restaurants, hotels, or dance places in Welholm Falls. No health clubs or indoor tennis centers. And a party in Welholm Falls was a summer barbecue or a potluck supper—the men played cribbage; the women discussed kids, blocking a new quilt, their husbands. His mom called Welholm Falls a simple place to live; his dad would call it boring.

Rob unfolded the paper, studied his dad's handwriting, the hurriedly written words. Besides being bored, his dad would call Welholm Falls a "jerkwater town," whatever that meant. Probably call the people "hicks." That's what his dad had called Jim when his mom announced that she was marrying a schoolteacher from Minnesota.

"I'll be in Minneapolis first week in February for important meeting. Will drive to Welholm Falls Saturday morning. Dad."

Rob ran his forefingers over the word *Dad*. Would he have changed? Would his mom be sorry she had left his dad?

Rob refolded the note, checked the calendar, counted the days. He drew a circle around the first Saturday in February, stared at it a long while and felt strangely detached from the man he was so anxious to see.

He had said good-bye to his dad last August. The past six months might as well have been six years. What would he say to his dad? Would his dad want to hear about Brian, about Jennifer—how she'd been taking piano lessons since she was six years old, about Smitty who wanted to grow up and be just like his dad, about

Doug who had enough trophies and ribbons to decorate a wall?

Probably not. Rob returned his dad's note to the desk drawer. He sat down, opened the geography book. "The Mississippi River roughly divides America in half, running from Minnesota to the Gulf of Mexico."

Rob's thoughts shifted off the page as he envisioned himself inside the *Ice Warrior*. He lined his craft at right angles to the wind, chose an imaginary point across the lake, and steered toward it. His best tacking speed was on a heading fifty-four degrees off the wind. Rob adjusted the sheet until the boat came about, then headed for the first marker on a long windward tack.

Mentally he went over the maneuver several times before it occurred to him that if he was going to get on the lake before dark, he needed to complete his homework and come up with an idea for his art project.

Jennifer had made a diorama of kids ice-skating; Smitty had handed in a model iceboat called *Winter Spirit*; Brian had made a salt-and-flour landscape of the lake and surrounding hills. Ms. Pickering had called them "creative."

Before Sunday ended, Rob managed a couple of hours on the lake with the *Ice Warrior*. He promised himself that for the rest of the week he'd get in an hour of practice each afternoon.

On Monday Ms. Pickering reminded him about the art project. Brian called him a few choice names because on Saturday he'd sailed off with Smitty to the east end of the lake instead of racing him.

On Thursday Jim drove to Demmering and returned

with enough cloth for a new sail. His mom began sewing Friday morning. Saturday noon, Rob telephoned Jennifer. "I have to take the *Ice Warrior* to the park's office for inspection. Want to ride along?"

Jennifer met him outside the boathouse twenty minutes later. "If you do any thing scary—"

"I give you my word." Rob closed the boathouse doors. "See how the seat widens out? Jim made it into a two-seater so you can ride with me."

Jennifer wound the tail of her long pink stocking cap around her neck. "Doesn't look all that extra wide to me."

Rob stepped back, waited until she slid down into the cockpit. "Hang on," he said, and released the parking brake. He took his place next to the cockpit on the windward side of the hull, took up the sheet, and held it taut. Rob pushed. He pushed until he could barely keep pace with the speed of his boat, then jumped on, slid down beside Jennifer. After drawing in the sheet, Rob adjusted his heading to sixty-five degrees, then decided upon the best tacking angle.

"You don't have to be afraid this time," he shouted. "I've been practicing."

Rob steered toward the north shore, pulled in on the sheet as he neared the inspection area, and took his place behind other boats waiting to be inspected.

"Hey"—the voice belonged to Brian—"look-y there."

Rob grimaced when he saw Brian, with Charlie Ellis leaning on his shoulder.

"The Junkman and his piece of junk."

Charlie Ellis laughed, called Rob's boat an orange fizzie.

Rob gave his helmet to Jennifer, stuffed the face mask inside. He wanted to throw back an insult, but what kind of bad thing could he say about a new boat?

The race inspector motioned Rob ahead, took the official papers, then flipped through the pages. "Nice-looking craft, Mr. Marshall. How does she handle?"

"Like a dream," Rob replied, catching a glimpse of Brian checking out the position of the runner plank.

"Hey," Brian yelled, "this ain't legal. It's too far back."

The inspector measured the distance between the runner plank and steering rudder. "A wrong distribution of weight will slow you down."

"But my boat will pass inspection, won't it?" Rob asked, catching Brian's smirk. Rob wanted to tell the inspector that the positioning of the runner plank had been Jim's idea, but before he could, the inspector's hand fell on his shoulder.

"Since this is your first race, maybe it's a good idea. Your craft might be a bit slower than the others, but it'll be safer for a beginner, provide more stability."

"Beginner!" Brian and Charlie hooted.

Had Jim purposely set the runner plank back to slow him down? Slow him down because he was a beginner? Rob waited for the inspector to sign the papers. "Take these to Mr. Hjelm. He's seated just inside the building, wearing a red coat. He'll assign you a number. Give you your DN letters."

Rob stuffed the papers into his pocket before moving

109

the *Ice Warrior* away from the inspection area. Brian and Charlie followed.

"Hey, Junkman, last place has your name on it."

Rob set the hand brake. "Watch my boat, will you, Jennifer?"

"Hurry. I'm cold."

Rob ran back to the office. He stopped just inside the building and in front of Mr. Hjelm's table. He took Rob's inspection papers, looked them over, then reached into a box for the numbers and letters. "The DN goes on both sides of the sail. Your number will be two twenty-two. Good luck."

The shiny sets of numbers and letters were black. Rob whirled around, in a rush to return to his boat.

"Young man"—a woman seated behind a second table motioned for Rob—"would you be a dear and pass out this bundle of posters around town and in your neighborhood?"

The posters of the determined and fierce-looking hockey player sat on the end of the table. Rob wanted to say no. There wasn't a fence, a telephone pole or store window in all of Welholm Falls that didn't already have at least two of the festival posters. But he said, "Sure," tucked the stack under his arm, and ran down the steps.

Brian and Charlie continued to hang around while Jennifer yelled at them to stop. "What's up?" Rob demanded.

"They've been climbing all over your boat and pulling on the ropes."

"Where did you get this stupid name?" Charlie demanded.

110

"It should be called the *Junk Boat*."

"Buzz off!" Rob shouted.

"Turn green," Brian fired back.

Rob felt blood rushing through his body, the adrenaline pumping, inciting his sense of justice. Keep on and I'll bust you both, Rob said inside his head as he pushed Brian from the runner plank.

"Watch it," Brian shouted, "or I'll fracture your earlobe."

"You and who else?" Rob yelled back. "And get your crummy hands off my sail."

Brian gave the sheet a hard jerk, looked back at Rob, challenging him. Jennifer pushed up inside the cockpit. "Come on, Rob. I have to get home. My mother—"

"Her mamma wants her," Brian mocked.

Rob dropped the bundle of posters. "Shut your face or I'll—" Rob moved closer.

A contemptuous sneer spread across Brian's face. "You're nothin' but talk, Junkman. You ain't got the—"

Rob dived at Brian, hit him in the belly with his shoulder, knocked him backward off the fuselage. Brian hit the ice first. Rob landed on top.

Jennifer screamed. Rob heard Brian yelling, heard Charlie's voice too. But he wasn't sure what they were saying; he didn't care. He just kept driving his fists into Brian's belly, against his shoulders, wherever they landed.

Some of the blows missed and went into the snow; some found Brian's chin or grazed his cheekbone, then Brian wiggled an arm free.

Churning and turning, one boy landed on top, then the other. Rob swung at Brian's chin, but Brian blocked the blow with a sharp elbow that slammed against Rob's forehead. For a second Rob couldn't see. He shook his head to clear the fuzziness that made his mind swirl.

"Charlie," Brian shouted, "get this maniac off of me."

"Hey." The inspector jerked Rob up. "For a skinny kid you're some kind of scrapper."

Rob stopped kicking when he saw blood on the snow, saw Brian holding his nose.

"He broke my nose," Brian yelled. "Gram's gonna sue you."

The inspector pulled Brian's hands away from his face. "Sorry to disappoint you, Brian, but your nose isn't broken. And no one I know of has ever sued over a bloody nose."

"They started it," Jennifer said, shaking her fist at Brian and Charlie. "They were climbing all over Rob's boat and trying to tear his sail."

"I think you boys should save your energy for the races."

Brian glared at Rob. "I'll beat you by ten miles, Marshall."

"You couldn't beat a turtle if you were jet propelled," Rob yelled back.

The inspector guided Rob into his cockpit. "I suggest you get the *Ice Warrior* home before those clouds settle in."

They were black clouds that reached the length of

the northern sky. "And you'd better not forget these."
The Inspector handed Rob the bundle of posters.

"Thanks for the push," Rob called back.

Rob took hold of the sheet. His legs gave every
indication of buckling as he pressed them around the
tiller. He'd never been in a real fight. Never hit anyone
out of anger. Dumb, he thought, but at the same time he
was glad—glad he'd fought Brian, glad he'd knocked
him down, bloodied his nose. So sue me!

Rob set a course for home. He didn't push the *Ice
Warrior* to go faster. He had this feeling—it wasn't a
scared feeling. Smart, maybe. A warning sense that told
him his brain and hands were not even close to function-
ing at the same speed.

Rob let out a deep sigh that was more of a body-
length shudder. It began between his shoulder blades,
then shot out in all directions, leaving his feet and
hands numb, his limbs quivering. Only his mind
seemed alive. And it kept projecting pictures of the
fight inside his head. Rob saw the right hand that he'd
landed on Brian's face and bloodied his nose. He saw
the picture over and over, saw it in slow motion too.
He was glad he hadn't broken Brian's nose, but he
wished that he'd landed a second punch that would
have blackened Brian's eye.

"Rob"—Jennifer finally spoke—"are you all right?
Your hands are shaking."

"I'm great," Rob answered. Then he glanced at Jennifer.

She looked scared, sort of pale inside all the pink

113

clothes. "No, I'm not great," he admitted. "I feel as if I'm gonna fall apart, and I don't like fighting."

"Did he hurt you?"

Rob felt his cheekbone, and Jennifer said, "It's awfully red. Bet you have a bruise tomorrow."

The spot stung, already felt the size of an egg. Probably be black and blue, and that ugly yellow, he thought. Would Brian's nose still show by Monday? Swollen, maybe, but Brian was sure to tell everyone that he'd won the fight.

CHAPTER 16

Monday morning turned out just as Rob expected: It was snowing again. There was not a single mark on Brian's face, while Rob wore a bruised splotch the size of a lopsided meatball. Brian's version of the fight made it sound as if Rob had failed to land a single punch.

Ms. Pickering reminded everyone about their art projects, repeating her threat to call the parents if the projects were late.

Would she? Would his mother tell his dad that his son was doing lousy in school? Would she ground him during Festival Weekend, stop him from participating in the race? Did he want to find out?

Just before Ms. Pickering dismissed class Thursday afternoon, she read off three names. "Sarah, Mark, and Rob Marshall have not turned in their art projects. If they are not on my desk by three o'clock tomorrow afternoon, I intend to make three telephone calls." She paused, looking from one student to another. "It would be a shame if the three of you were to miss Winter Festival. Class dismissed."

Rob shot out of the room first, then out of the building into the snowy afternoon. "Tomorrow." He repeated the word several more times. "Tomorrow I have to turn in an art project. Tomorrow!"

But what? Rob slid around the corner at Lakefront; he saw Ms. Johannsen getting into Jim's car and remembered that Jennifer's mom worked Thursday evenings at the library and that his parents had an appointment in Loganna with the man who was preparing their income tax returns.

Rob found a note on the kitchen table—dinner was in the oven. He munched on a lemon cookie as he climbed the stairs. Music from Doug's stereo filled the hallway. Rob dropped his books on the desk. The bundle of festival posters he'd been asked to distribute around town stared back at him. He turned the faces of the fierce-looking hockey players against the wall, then watched the snow falling outside his bedroom window.

The path to the boathouse was covered over. The garden plot rested beneath a three-foot blanket. Every limb on the leafless maple in the backyard was outlined with snow. Next fall he intended to do something with the leafless maple, like . . . something clicked inside Rob's brain. It clicked a second time, and he spun around. He picked up and studied a poster. Asked himself, why not?

But which one? The one at school? Rob spread the posters around the room. "Downtown, maybe?"

Rob grabbed a pair of scissors from his desk drawer.

116

He cut a fierce-looking hockey player from the center of thirty-one festival posters. He painted the back side of each with watercolors. He did stripes and bold zigzags, a few solids. "With the Christmas lights burning and the snow, they'll look sensational," he said.

"Hey"—Doug poked his head inside Rob's room— "let's eat."

First Doug, then Rob rode the banister downstairs. "Will you be okay here alone?" Doug asked. "I'm meeting a couple of girls at the library to study for a trig exam."

They ate quickly. Each rinsed his own plate and silverware before depositing them in the dishwasher. "See you."

Rob waved. He ran upstairs. He finished painting the cutouts. He used an ice pick to put a hole in the top of each, then laced a length of his mom's green yarn through the eye. He stood back to admire his work. He knew Ms. Pickering would like his idea. She was always talking about originality and initiative.

Rob wore his parka, face mask, and gloves. He paused at the back door long enough to slip into rubber boots. Light snow continued to fall. An occasional car passed on the street. It was a perfect night, quiet and stormy. Tomorrow, all of Welholm Falls would wake up and find his tree. They would talk about it, photograph it, make bets on who had done it. Rob grinned. Ms. Pickering would drive right past it on her way to school. She would see the tree right off. She might even steer her car up onto the curb or bump into another car because she would be so busy admiring it.

Rob chuckled and hurried on toward the center of

town. The stores were dark, the street empty. Rob shifted his load to the other arm. The first tree in the parkway had to be a hundred years old. The trunk was bigger around than his mother's laundry basket. But Rob passed it up for the old maple tree that faced the park's office.

He stepped back from the tree, studied it, and decided on the branches that would best show off the cutouts. He would have to be careful and hang the hockey players close to a cluster of tree lights, which would flash on and off. People would see the unusual decorations and move in for a closer look. "Neat," Rob whispered. "Great idea."

He reached for the first limb. Climbing trees was summer fun. In the winter a ladder and flashlight would have been a help. Rob inched his way up, careful to avoid tangling a foot in the light cords.

He hung a cutout on the highest limb first, stretched up as high as he could reach, tied the player to the branch with green yarn, then climbed down.

"Rob . . ." The voice came out of the darkness. "Rob Marshall, is that you?"

"Ms. Johannsen?"

"What in heaven's name are you doing? It's freezing out here."

Rob hesitated. Should he tell her the truth or make up an excuse? "I'm doing my art project."

"You're doing what?" She crossed the street.

"It's a Winter Festival art project that Ms. Pickering assigned."

Rob held out one of the cutouts. Ms. Johannsen asked, "How many more do you have to hang?"

"Thirty."

She repeated the number. "Well, you had better hurry. It's getting colder by the minute, and Officer Lindstrom makes his nightly rounds at ten-thirty."

"Good thing you came along. I might have ended up in jail."

"I'm sure that would please your parents."

"You don't have to hang around," Rob said. "I'll be okay."

But Jennifer's mother waited, keeping Rob posted on the time and handing up the cutouts. "Farther out on the end of the limb," she advised, "or the tree will look one-sided."

Rob followed her instructions until the last decoration hung in place. "What time is it?"

"A quarter past ten."

Rob dropped to the ground. "I sure hope Ms. Pickering likes my project."

"What type of paint did you use?" She pointed to the colored snow.

Rob studied the splotches of watercolor paint.

"It's too late to do anything now," she said. "That's Officer Lindstrom's car at the end of the block."

Rob groaned. He fell in at Ms. Johannsen's side. His great and different idea might end up a great and messy fizzle. "Dang it," he said. "How come nothing ever turns out exactly like a fellow plans?"

All day Friday, Rob waited for Ms. Pickering to mention the tree in front of the park's office but she said nothing until five minutes before three. "Rob, do you have your project completed and ready to turn in?"

119

Rob's mouth dropped open. Did that mean . . . you mean that . . . limpin' lizards, hadn't she seen it?

"Well?" Ms. Pickering asked.

"I finished it." Rob stood. He glanced around the room.

His classmates waited for an explanation too. Rob took a deep breath. He began telling how he had decorated the tree with cutouts from the festival posters. "I did it last night just before Officer Lindstrom made his ten-thirty rounds."

"You may sit down."

Did she believe him? Rob couldn't be certain. He stayed after class and when the room was empty, he said, "I wanted to do something really different. I had to wait until the last minute." Rob looked down at his shoes, bit the inside of his cheek. "That's not true. I didn't get the whole idea until yesterday afternoon."

"I'll check your work on my way home. And, Rob," she said, "I agree; it is a different idea."

"Then it's okay?"

She smiled. "Art is an expression of one's imagination. I'm impressed." She came from behind her desk. "It looks as if we'll have clear weather for tomorrow. Hope you have good luck with your iceboat."

"Thanks, and don't forget the amateur race starts at two sharp. My dad's going to be here. He's driving up from Minneapolis in the morning. Mom's going to invite him for dinner tomorrow night too. See you, Ms. Pickering."

Rob found Jennifer waiting outside. "Is she mad at you?"

120

Rob shook his head. "She's impressed with my imagination. She even wished me good luck for tomorrow's race."

Jennifer carefully arranged her blond hair beneath the pink stocking cap. "I heard Brian tell Charlie he was going to go look at your 'crummy tree.' Do you think he'll try and pull off the decorations before Ms. Pickering gets to see them?"

"Not in broad daylight he won't, and Ms. Pickering said she'd stop and look at them on her way home." Rob tucked his rubber boots under his arm. "It's stopped snowing. It's supposed to be really nice tomorrow. Windy, but the sun's going to shine."

Rob laughed. "My dad probably brought the good weather with him from California. He's in Minneapolis today."

"You want to come along with Mother and me to the church potluck tonight? Your parents and my father are going to a meeting."

"Better not. I have to put the DN letters on my sail. My dad will be here early in the morning. Maybe before daylight."

Rob grinned. "I can hardly wait to see him. You've got to meet him, Jennifer. You're really gonna like him. Maybe we can all have lunch together."

Jennifer turned up her drive. "See you tomorrow, Rob. I hope you beat Brian . . . everyone else too."

"I will," Rob called back. "I'm going to win by a mile."

CHAPTER 17

Rob opened one eye, focused on the clock radio, the luminous green dials. *Limpin' lizards! Five-thirty*. He jumped from bed. His dad might very well be outside waiting. Rob ran to the window, looked down on the empty driveway, then gathered up his clothes and hurried down the hall. He brushed his teeth, showered, and dressed in record time. Though the amateur iceboat races were not scheduled until 2:00, he wanted to be ready when his dad drove up to the front of the house. He wanted to take his dad to the pancake breakfast, introduce him to Jennifer and Ms. Pickering, show him the tree in front of the park's office, show him the *Ice Warrior*.

Rob ate cold cereal and drank hot chocolate between trips to the bow window that looked out onto Lakefront Drive. Blue sky and sunshine eliminated the possibilities of his dad running into road closures. And the local weatherman predicted temperatures in the low teens, clear skies with light wind, gusts in the afternoon. Rob switched off the radio. Light wind would be no problem for his dad driving to Welholm Falls, but afternoon gusts meant trouble for the *Ice Warrior*. As Rob stepped backward toward the kitchen, he thought about the race, the effects of the wind, and the necessary precautions. This would be his first race. The *Ice Warrior* was an almost new boat. There were things he didn't know. Instead of worrying about those things, Rob shifted his attention to the wall clock, then back to his dad's note: "Saturday morning."

Rob understood that *early* to him might mean something different to his dad. And Rob continued to wait.

Jim left to referee the Junior League hockey game at 7:30. Doug left a half hour later. And at 9:00 Rob's mom kissed him on the cheek and said, "I'm working the coffee booth this morning so I'll be free to see you win the amateur race. I'll be back about noon, so please leave the back door unlocked when you go."

"Mom, are you sure it's okay with Jim for me to invite Dad to stay for dinner?"

She slipped into her coat, gave Rob a hug. "I'm sure. We'll eat around six o'clock."

Rob followed her into the garage. "Do you think maybe Dad could have had car trouble? Maybe he got in an accident. Jeez, Mom, this is the longest morning I've ever lived."

She smiled as if she understood. "Did he say where he was staying in Minneapolis? You could call."

"He just said he was there for a meeting, that he would rent a car early this morning and drive up."

She slid behind the steering wheel, blew Rob a kiss. "I love you," she called, and left Rob to wait alone.

Nine-thirty.

Ten. The telephone rang, but it was a wrong number.

Ten-thirty. Rob ran upstairs, found his thermal underwear, new wool socks, fleecy glove liners. He carried them downstairs, set his boots beside the heat register to warm.

Eleven-thirty. Rob walked out to the garage, left the door open so he could still hear the telephone if it rang. He looked toward the corner. Maybe his dad was lost; maybe he had misplaced the address. But there were telephone books. Rob returned to the pile of woolen clothes in front of the bow window. He sat down. Part of him wanted to cry. Part of him fought back.

When his mother returned at 12:15, Rob said, "I don't care if he comes. I don't need him. I'm glad he's not here!"

But with the angry outburst there were tears, stinging ones that originated from the pain in Rob's heart. Then his mom's arms went around him. He smelled her perfume, the hint of pancakes and coffee. He felt her warmth and when she said, "I know how badly it hurts," he knew that she knew.

She pushed him away, took his hand, led him to the sofa, and drew him down beside her. "You have something very important to do today, something that's going to take all of your determination and total concentration. When it's over, when you walk up to claim your trophy, you're going to know just how courageous Rob Marshall really is."

She squeezed his hand inside hers. "From that moment on, you will always know, no matter the job before you, that you can do it, do anything you set your mind to doing."

She raised her hand to his face, held his gaze inside of hers. "Do you understand what I'm saying?"

"Why couldn't he have come? I wanted him to see me race, see me win. Mom, I've practiced so hard. I just wanted him to be really proud of me."

"Rob, you don't have to win a race to make someone proud of you."

"With Dad you do." Rob looked down at his feet. "Remember he used to say, 'Winning isn't everything, Rob. It's the only thing'?"

"Listen to me, Robert Marshall. You *are* a winner. Jim says that you have more courage than any boy he's ever known."

Rob stood, stepped away from his mother. "What does it mean to be your own person?"

"It means knowing who and what you are, rather than doing things to prove to others who and what you are. You don't have to win, Rob, for us to be proud of you. We're very proud of you and all that you've done since you came here last August." Her voice softened. "You're a very courageous person. Don't you know that about yourself?"

After a moment, Rob said, "I guess."

"Good. Now let's have lunch."

He followed slowly behind, sat on the stool, and watched her start the oven. "Maybe I should run down to the boathouse and get the *Ice Warrior* onto the ice."

"Better hurry. It won't take long to heat up this pizza I brought home."

"Pizza? You brought home a pizza?"

"Mushroom and double cheese."

"My favorite. Mom—"

Before Rob finished his question, the telephone rang. She picked it up. "Hello. Yes, just a minute."

The tone of her voice, the tightly drawn lips told Rob who it was before she said, "It's your dad."

Rob took the receiver. "Hi, Dad. Where are you? How come you're so late?"

"How you doing, Son? You sound all grown up."

"I'm doing okay. Where are you? The race starts at two."

"Listen, Rob, I'm not going to make it this weekend. I'm at the airport here in Minneapolis waiting for a flight to Detroit. I have a Monday morning appointment with some really important clients and I need time to go over my presentation. I've been working on this account two years, Rob, and I think I can get them to sign this time. I'll make it up to you. I'll get back up here as soon as I can break away. I promise."

Rob bit down on the edge of his lip until the pain made him forget his dad's voice.

"Sure, Dad." But Rob stopped listening. The swelling inside his heart threatened to choke him. He told his dad good-bye, hung up the telephone, then looked at his mom, looked at her through wet and blurry eyes.

"He's not coming," Rob whispered. "A big deal with some really important people in Detroit on Monday. Mom . . ."

She grabbed him, hugged him. "Rob Marshall"— she almost yelled—"you're going to do just fine today. Do you hear me, you're going to win!"

She held him an arm's length away. "I've never been on an iceboat but Jim says you're a good pilot. I would appreciate a ride to the park. And if we leave right now, I'll buy hot dogs and apple dumplings. Is it a deal?"

Rob blinked aside his tear. "Deal," he said, and slapped his mom's outstretched hands.

CHAPTER 18

At 1:30 Rob pushed the *Ice Warrior* toward the starting area. Hundreds of spectators crowded both sides of the marker buoys—his mom, Jim, Jennifer, and Ms. Pickering. He saw her talking with his mom. Was she telling her that he'd failed, that his art project was a fizzle? Rob maneuvered the *Ice Warrior* into line. He set the hand brake, backed off a few steps to admire his boat's sleek new fuselage, the sail his mother had made. Lots of people had helped him. Jim said it was his determination that made the *Ice Warrior*. Rob had never thought of himself in such big words . . . his determination. A sense of pride and accomplishment welled up within Rob until he heard Brian Sass laugh.

Charlie Ellis, Brian, Jerry Canady—all winners of the morning's hockey championship game. Brian called Rob's boat *Junk Bucket* so everyone would hear. Rob followed him a few steps, his hands drawn up into tight fists, but it was Jennifer yelling, "Hurry up, Rob," that made him stop, consider. They might be laughing now, but just wait.

"I have something to give you," Jennifer called. When Rob reached the rope that held back the spectators, Jennifer thrust a rabbit's foot into his hand. "Father gave it to me just before my first recital. It's for special good luck."

Ms. Pickering said, "I'm proud of you. Your art project was among the best."

Jim winked. His mother smiled. And Doug said, "Dad's always wanted a kid with artistic talent."

Rob blinked. He looked at his mom, Doug, back to his new dad, then Jennifer. Before he could put his thoughts into words, Ms. Pickering drew him aside. "The paint on your cutouts ran all over everything, but when it did, it made multicolored icicles that are beautiful with the sunlight reflecting through them." Ms. Pickering bent closer. "I'm betting Mr. Enge supper that you'll win this race."

"You're betting on me to win?"

"You did tell me you were the best windsurfer in San Diego, didn't you?"

"Sure, but I sort of . . . Well, maybe I stretched the truth some."

The whistle sounded; the loudspeaker crackled on. "All iceboat pilots entered in the amateur DN division, man your boats."

Rob ran the short distance. He turned suddenly cold. "All right," the starter called. "I want you young men to obey all the rules and show good sportsmanship. Remember: Watch for boats in trouble. I'll begin the count in just a few seconds."

The amateur boats formed a straight line across the ice, their steering runners on the starting line. Fifteen feet separated each boat. "Ready," the starter ordered. "We'll begin with the count of ten. The gun will go off on zero. Good luck."

Rob pulled on his face mask, his goggles, his helmet. He felt the rabbit's foot in his jacket pocket. And the countdown began. "Ten."

Each pilot stood at the rear of his boat, rocking it back and forth to keep the runners from freezing. "Nine. Eight."

Rob tried to swallow. His windpipe felt frozen shut. "Seven."

"Six."

"Five."

Rob glanced down the line. Smitty waited on the far right. Charlie and Brian held positions near the opposite end.

"Four."

"Three."

"Two."

"Limpin' lizards." Rob gulped.

"One."

The gun went off. Each pilot ran his boat out onto the course, and when Rob was satisfied with his boat's speed, he leaped into the cockpit, letting the sail fill and the wind take charge.

It was a long quarter-mile to the first marker, and the boats began to string out. Rob figured he was somewhere in the middle. The wind picked up, pushed harder. Rob watched the telltale carefully, always allowing for a slight luff. No unexpected gust was going to wipe him out of this race.

Rob maneuvered past several slower boats but the ones in the lead pressed farther ahead. The *Ice Warrior* wasn't the fastest boat on the course. It had to be the position of the runner plank that slowed him down and Rob was disappointed. Jim must have known it would cut his speed.

Rob yelled a curse and hauled the sail in close. The *Ice Warrior* leaped ahead. He swung the steering runner toward the shoreline as another boat loomed up in his path. The *Ice Warrior* shot past, picked up additional speed under the taut sail. Twenty, thirty miles an hour, Rob judged, and sank lower in the cockpit. The wind was shattering. He felt the cold, the splinters of ice pricking through the flannel-lined face mask. He knew what a sudden side-gust might do, but if he was to win, he couldn't pilot a safe race. In an instant he decided. He veered the steering shaft to starboard.

The razor-sharp front runner swung the *Ice Warrior* back toward the course markers. Rob glanced around; the boat he had just passed faded quickly, yet he continued to lose ground to the leaders. He scooted forward. "Come on. Come on."

He had to gain speed on this downwind tack. With an eye on the telltale and slowly drawing in the sheet,

Rob felt the wind tear at his parka. The honed runners skimmed across greenish gray ice while the wind snapped at the sail, and the *Ice Warrior* left a jetlike *swoosh* in its wake.

The ride was smooth. The speed made Rob catch his breath. The *Ice Warrior* was flying, banked to port. The boat careened across the frozen surface on two runners. He went rigid before he was able to shake aside the fear.

"Easy. Easy," he muttered, and eased out the sheet, dumping only enough wind to settle the boat back onto three runners.

Still, he had lost speed. Slowly he drew the sheet taut. Wind nipped at the cloth like a whipcrack. The boat picked up speed, barely touching the ice as it rocketed toward the halfway marker and a cluster of boats.

He closed on them rapidly. The uncertain wind was giving them problems too, hiking their crafts, causing them to sail scared. Rob swung the steering shaft to port and circled the group. Once he drew back into the downwind tack, the *Ice Warrior* sped ahead, narrowing the gap on another boat.

The wind increased. Rob watched the telltale, watched the boats ahead, his fingers cramped around the sheet, holding it tight. Each time the wind snapped against the sail, Rob eased out on the sheet, controlling his speed, preventing a hike. With the winds and fierce gusts, Rob sensed that his boat had better stability than the others. He understood now why Jim had set the runner plank back those few inches. It allowed Rob that extra split second he needed to luff his sail. While the other pilots fought the gusty, unpredictable winds, Rob sped ahead.

He passed Charlie Ellis, moved up on Smitty's *Windy Demon*. Rob maneuvered *Ice Warrior* around the required side of the marker buoy. Brian's *Annihilator* ran just ahead. Rob recognized Brian's red helmet, the white telltale ribbons trailing out from his bowstay.

"Come on. Come on," Rob shouted, aware he was pressing. If a gust hit the *Ice Warrior* now, with every inch of its cloth catching the wind. . . . Rob gulped. He would end up on the bottom of a three-sixty capsize. But to overtake the *Annihilator* he had to take the chance, and slowly, Rob drew in the sheet.

Rob chased after the *Annihilator*, leaving Smitty and the others far behind. Slowly the distance between Brian's boat and the *Ice Warrior* lessened. Rob felt the *Ice Warrior* shudder—thirty, thirty-five, then forty. He fought to keep his boat in proper trim, watched the telltale for the slightest shift as the wind continued to gust out of the northwest.

Rob checked the telltale, then stole a quick peek to check the *Annihilator*'s position.

"Limpin' lizards!" Rob yelled. The *Annihilator* was in a midair capsize. "Lean to port," Rob shouted. "Lean to port."

Brian's new DN tipped farther and farther until it flipped over like a wounded bird. The mast snapped. The fuselage skidded, slid, veering right, before throwing Brian free. His body bent, he hit the ice, and seemed to slide forever before finally stopping.

The *Ice Warrior* closed in. "Get up," Rob shouted. "Get up, loudmouth. Get up!"

Brian remained motionless on the ice.

"Get up," Rob screamed. "Get up."

Once again, he heard his dad say: "Winning isn't everything. It's the only thing." But then, deep in his mind, he heard his own voice cry out: "You're wrong, Dad, dead wrong!"

Rob dumped the wind. The *Ice Warrior* came about, skidding to an abrupt stop. Rob set his hand brake, jumped from the cockpit. He set the parking brake before racing across the ice.

Brian's eyes were closed. Blood wet the chin of his face mask. Rob knelt at Brian's side, loosened his helmet, pulled it off, removed the face mask. Blood seeped from a deep cut across Brian's chin. He moaned. His eyelids lifted, fell shut, lifted again. He stared at Rob, shook his head, blinked.

"You okay?" Rob asked. "You know where you are?"

Brian shook his head several more times before he sat up. He looked around, pulled free of Rob's steadying grip. He rose onto his knees, crawled forward a few feet, moaned a low, painful sound.

"Yeah," Rob said. "Your new boat is a disaster."

Smitty's *Windy Demon* swooshed past, and Charlie Ellis followed as Brian leaned back on his heels. He looked at Rob, then his eyes narrowed into a tight, critical stare. "You're dumb, a real dumbhead." He stood, wavering unsteadily. "You could have won. I wouldn't have stopped for you."

"I know," Rob answered. "Winning is all that matters to you. But I'm not you. You want me to help you get your boat back to the starting area?"

"I don't need your help. I don't need anyone's help—you got that, Junkman?"

As Rob returned to the *Ice Warrior*, he heard a sound that made him wonder if Brian was crying—or was it just the wind?

CHAPTER 19

Jennifer waited while Rob crawled under the rope that held back the spectators. When he held out the rabbit's foot to give it back, Jennifer said, "It's for you to keep forever."

"I could have won," Rob said.

Jennifer smiled and pulled on Rob's arm.

"Where are we going?" he asked.

Before Jennifer could answer, Ms. Pickering intercepted them. "I'm sorry about your bet," Rob said. "I'd offer to cook Mr. Enge supper except he might not like frozen pizza."

"Don't you dare apologize. I may have to cook Mr. Enge supper, but I placed my bet on the winner."

Rob followed behind Jennifer and at Ms. Pickering's side. "Where are we going?" he asked.

"Your parents are holding seats for us. You do want to see the presentation ceremonies, don't you?"

Rob shrugged. He would rather have gone home, but he took the empty seat alongside his mother and next to Jennifer. His mother gave him a hug. It was a special kind of hug she saved for really tragic times, like the night his dad had had to rush off to attend an important business meeting instead of visiting school to see Rob play Joseph in the Christmas program.

Rob took a long, deep breath. Maybe it was better that his dad had chosen to go on to Detroit. After all, excuses were for losers.

Jim leaned over, placed a hand on Rob's knee. "You did a very unselfish thing out there."

Before Rob could reply, the festival chairman stepped onstage, raising a hand for quiet. He made a short speech as he handed out each of the trophies. Smitty, Jerry, Charlie, and Brian all won hockey ribbons. Smitty cradled the tall, iceboating trophy, and Charlie Ellis won second place. Doug won a trophy for being the most valuable player in Junior League hockey. And Rob heard his mother tell Ms. Pickering, "Doug is sure to win that scholarship now."

At the conclusion of the ceremonies, Rob wandered back to the *Ice Warrior*. He sat on the runner plank. "I sure let you down," he whispered. "You could have won if I'd just been—"

"Maybe you could have won"—Jim's long shadow fell across the ice at Rob's feet—"but you're not a loser."

Rob cupped his hands around his mouth and blew his warm breath against his fingers. "I sure wanted to win one of the trophies for the shelf at home."

"You won something more than a trophy, Rob." Jim sat next to Rob on the runner plank. "And what about this? I think it's as important as a trophy."

Jim held out a stiff piece of paper. "The city council has awarded you first place for the best piece of original artwork."

Rob fought to hold back his amazement as he stared at the square of paper. First place? Well . . . that was something anyway. Well . . . that was *really* something. Rob smiled tentatively at Jim, who looked very proud.

"Hey, Marshall." The voice came from nowhere.

Rob wrenched around. Brian Sass . . . Charlie Ellis . . . Smitty . . . Jerry Canady. . . . Brian motioned for Rob. "Us guys are going for pizza. If you want to come along, it's okay."

Rob turned to ask his dad. "Go ahead, Son. Doug and I'll take the *Ice Warrior* home."

Rob ran to catch up. Smitty threw an arm around Rob's shoulders. "You know, guys," Smitty said, "I think we ought to let Rob choose the pizza."

"Nothing doing," Brian yelled. "It's my turn to choose."

"That's okay by me," Rob said, skipping every couple of steps to keep up with the other guys' longer strides.